Mean Sea Level

Enjoy the beach!

Pat Heaney

Pat Heaney

Mean Sea Level

ISBN-13: 978-0-988478-6-6
ISBN-10: 0988847868

Riding the Waves Publishing

Acknowledgements

I owe much to the members of the Belmar Arts Council Writer's Critique Group led by the wonderful Cindy Dunn. I want to thank Jane McCullough for her very thorough editing, and Lauren Griffin and Beth Worton, my beta readers.

I could not have completed this project without the multi-talented Merry Brennan and Freda Karpf at Riding the Waves Publishing. Special thanks to Chloe and Phoebe for posing for the cover art and to Jon Gibbs for tons of advice, some of which I actually heeded. I am full of gratitude and love for my biggest supporter: my amazing husband, Dan McCullough

Chapter 1

"What are you doing, Peggy? Stay away from my stuff!" My sister Linda walked in and caught me just as I was smoothing her bed ruffle back into place.

"Nothing, I'm just looking for my flip flops." I stood up and pushed my way past her to look under the dresser we shared. Linda was 15, nearly three years older than me, and she made it abundantly clear that she hated sharing the room with me.

"They're not in here, dork. Why can't you just walk to the beach without them like everyone else?" She called after me as I ran down the stairs to look on the first floor.

I wouldn't mind walking to the beach barefoot; it was the boardwalk I was afraid of. It was rough and splintery, and I was bound to get a sliver in the bottom of my foot. I looked around the living and dining rooms and finally found my yellow flip flops right next to the back door. I slipped them on and ran outside to meet my friends, Suzy Blankenship and Colleen McMann.

Although we had only been out of school for a couple of weeks, we were well into the summer routine. Suzy and I met up in the empty lot between our houses. We had our swim suits under our shorts and draped our beach towels around our necks. My flip flops clicked along as we crossed the street to pick up Colleen, who was waiting on her wrap-around front porch. Colleen started down the wooden porch stairs then halted mid-step.

"Oh no! I forgot my pocketbook, wait for me!" She ran back into the house. The aluminum screen door took its time closing behind her with a slow hush of air.

"Geez Colleen, you and that stupid pocketbook." Suzy was already starting to walk away. "You think you're so mature." Of course, Colleen couldn't hear any of this, because she was in her house retrieving her ever-present straw purse.

I stood on the sidewalk unsure whether to wait for Colleen, or go ahead with Suzy, who was already halfway down the block. Before I could make my decision, Colleen popped back out the front door and flew down the steps right past me to catch up with Suzy. I was a slow runner, and the flip flops didn't help matters. I huffed and puffed along until I caught up with the two of them, now walking together along the sidewalk.

As we strolled the remaining four blocks to the ocean we passed several people that we knew and a few we didn't really know, but saw on the street nearly every day. Over time we had concocted stories and names for all of them.

"Here comes Old Moses," Suzy said when she saw the guy we secretly called Moses Walker coming up the block.

"Ew, he's gross. I would never date a man with a beard," Colleen asserted.

Moses had long blonde hair and a big beard and walked through our neighborhood daily. He was very tall with long legs that appeared even longer because of the skimpy gym shorts he always wore. He moved very quickly and smoothly with great strides. Moses always seemed to be looking up at the sky, deep in thought. He never spoke to us; I wondered if he even noticed us.

"Don't be such a baby Colleen; he keeps all kinds of good stuff in that beard: money, diamonds, candy. I'll bet he's got a bag of M&M's in there right now. You should go stick your hand in and get some."

"Shut up, Suzy; don't gross me out so early in the morning." Colleen said then quickly changed the subject, "Oh, look they're wearing red today!" she pointed to a couple jogging up the street in matching track suits. The man had dark hair and a big bushy mustache. His wife was very thin with red curls that she kept out of her face with a wide stretchy hair band. Her cheeks were usually as red as her hair. They had three different running suits: red, blue and grey, with white stripes down the legs and arms. Every day their colors matched. If he wore blue, so did she. They jogged, not on the sidewalk, but in the road, side by side. They would usually smile or give us a little wave, sometimes the woman would manage to say "good morning" between her ragged breaths. Because of their track suits, we called them the Stripers. I admit, the names were not all that creative, but we came up with some great stories about them that would constantly change.

"Did you know that the Stripers used to be spies in Russia," I offered "They had to crawl through underground caves to bring their secrets back to the US government."

Colleen picked up the thread. "That's how they first met. A Russian threw acid in Mrs. Striper's eyes and she couldn't see, so Mr. Striper rescued her and carried her into the caves. She had never even seen what he looked like, but they fell in love while they made their way to safety. When she finally got the bandages off her eyes, it was love at first sight." Colleen sighed.

"There were chimp monkeys in the cave and Mrs. Striper thought that one of the monkeys was Mr. Striper, cause of his big hairy mustache." Suzy jumped in "So she's making out with the monkey for like ten minutes until Striper comes back from taking a piss and finds her kissing the chimp."

"God, Suzy! Do you have to be so crude?" Colleen said.

This was the way our stories went. I usually liked to imagine them as spies, or lost royalty. It was the early 1970's so whenever we needed a bad guy, naturally he was Russian. Nothing was scarier than the Soviet Union. Colleen liked to tell stories about their love lives which Suzy would turn into bizarre and usually disgusting tales.

As Suzy was still going on about the Stripers and the slave monkeys in their cellar, I spotted someone new crossing Third Avenue half a block in front of us. A teen girl, or maybe a young woman; I couldn't quite tell. She was slim and graceful with long straight dark hair pulled into a fat braid down her back. She was carrying some sort of large bag over her shoulder, but it was hard to see from where we stood. I thought there was something special about this girl, something about the way she walked down the street, like her feet weren't quite touching the ground. I stared for a moment. I was about to point her out to Suzy and Colleen, but stopped myself. I didn't want them giving her a wacky name, or making up a story about her. I didn't want them to ruin her. Instead, I asked Suzy if the Stripers had any other pets. This lead to a hilarious description of the chickens they kept in their pantry.

We reached the ocean then took the boardwalk north to our preferred beach.

"Let's hop down here and walk on the sand," Suzy said. She was always willing to break the rules and jump over the rail down to the sand instead of going through the badge checker and down the stairs.

"I want to go down to the second entrance and see if Chris is working," Colleen was becoming a bit boy crazy. Her latest crush was Christopher Flynn, a 15 year old who worked checking beach badges.

"Ugh, forget it, Colleen, he's at least two years older than you" I did not want to see him or his bossy sisters, Kerry and Kelly.

"C'mon, he is so cute!"

By this time Suzy was already climbing over the rail and I had to decide whether to follow her or continue down the boardwalk to look for Christopher. It seemed like nearly every day I was in a position like this. Always torn between the two of them, with neither choice being the one I really wanted. As usual, I took the safe and law abiding way and followed Colleen down to the stairway. In order to get to Christopher's regular post we had to pass right by one entrance, where some old guy always sat checking badges.

The badge checkers sat on green wooden rocking chairs at each of the stairways that led from the boardwalk down to the sand. Their job was to make sure that nobody snuck onto the beach without showing a beach badge. They each had a chalkboard on which they could write the water temperature and the time of the next high tide. Most of them kept their chalkboards pretty simple, but the old man at the first staircase always added a daily quote to his board. I don't know if anybody else bothered to read it, but I would usually glance at it. Today it read:

Life shrinks or expands in proportion
to one's courage. Anais Nin.
H2O Temp 67 Low Tide 12:20.

Most of the badge checkers were retirees or school teachers on summer break. Somehow Christopher Flynn managed to get a summer job doing it. His parents were well known in the town and had probably gotten it for him. Tall and athletic, his head was covered with loose blond curls that fell down around his small eyes. Colleen thought he was really handsome, but to me he had a sort of dull look about him, like there wasn't much going on in his head. I never told Col that I thought he just looked dumb.

The Flynns lived just a few blocks from the beach in a newish house. His family owned a real estate agency and a travel agency in town. His twin sisters were in my grade; but were stuck up and rarely spoke to me. They missed a lot of school to go on trips. They went skiing every winter and always left the lift tags on their jacket zippers afterwards so that everyone knew where they had been. For some reason this drove me crazy.

Christopher was sitting in his green rocking chair guarding the steps to the boardwalk. He was reading some kind of magazine. He barely looked up when I walked by and pointed to the season badge that was pinned to my shorts. Colleen made a point of stopping and taking her badge out of her oh-so-sophisticated purse to show it to him. She got no more of a reaction than I did.

"See you later, Chris" she warbled.

"Yep", he mumbled.

The regulars on the beach were already in their usual spots. The smell of coconut tanning oil mingled with the salty scent of the sea. On any weekday you could predict who would be there and where they'd be sitting. The moms with the little kids and giant striped umbrellas sat nearest to the big wooden lifeguard stands. The old people in folding chairs and hats sat near the shade of the boardwalk. Each group had an area that they called their own. There were no markers or signs, but we all just knew. On weekends, all bets were off. The weekend people had no clue about the order of things; they plopped down wherever they wanted, often sitting entirely too close. The beach got way too crowded on Saturdays and Sundays and we usually didn't even bother to go.

Colleen and I ran across the hot sand to our regular spot where Suzy had already spread out her towel.

"You comin' out?"

"Yep, wait for me," I replied, as Suzy was already running down to the water's edge.

Suzy was short and thin with blonde hair and green eyes. Her head was covered with cowlicks that made her straight, fine hair stick out wildly in several different directions. She didn't spend much time on her appearance; her ragamuffin looks suited her.

"I'll be out a little later, I want to work on my tan." Colleen was busy applying a mixture of baby oil and iodine to her already tanned skin.

At the beach "out" meant into the water and "in" meant out of the surf, back up onto the sand. No one questioned this or thought of it as odd phrasing. It made complete sense to us.

Suzy and I spend most of the day out, with Colleen taking occasional swims followed by a great deal of time spent brushing her long honey colored hair. Colleen was the tallest of the three of us. She had an athletic build and was just on the edge of being fat; I guessed that was why she always wore a one piece swimsuit. Her purse contained all the things a sophisticated nearly 13-year old girl needed at the beach: brush, comb, tanning lotion, chewing gum, tissues, lip gloss and a small beaded coin purse. I, on the other hand, brought nothing but my towel; not even a comb in my pocket. If I was lucky I'd have a few quarters or a folded up dollar bill to spend on french fries or ice cream.

Colleen was the only one of us who got a weekly allowance for doing her chores. I made money by babysitting some of the neighborhood kids. The going rate was $1.00 an hour. I would usually watch the kids for a few hours in the evening while their parents went out to dinner. Suzy sometimes babysat, but usually she would get money from her Uncle. If she kept him company for a little while, he would give her a couple of dollars. I didn't quite understand the relationship, but I didn’t have any uncles.

By early afternoon we were done with the beach and headed back home. When we got to our block we split up and went our separate ways with plans to meet up the next morning.

CHAPTER 2

I would always go home and squirt myself off with the garden hose before changing out of my wet swimsuit. When I got to the backyard my big sister Linda and her best friend Cindy Blankenship, who was Suzy's older sister, were lounging on beach chairs listening to a transistor radio and looking at magazines.

"Hey Piggy, don't get sand all over the house" Linda never seemed to tire of picking on me.

"Shove it" was my only reply and I obediently rinsed off before going in.

I made my usual lunch of a peanut butter and jelly sandwich. I suppose it would be more properly called peanut butter and preserves. Each summer my mother put up strawberry preserves. I helped her sort through big trays of fresh berries picked from the back yard garden. The kitchen filled with the hot steam rising from the giant blue speckled canning pot; the scent of sweet berries and sugar made my mouth water. Mom would lift the shining glass jars from the vat of water and line them up along the counter. We carefully checked all the jars to make sure the lids were properly sealed. Any jars that didn't pass inspection were put in the refrigerator; we could eat these right away. Even in the middle of the winter, the scent of strawberry preserves would take me right back to that steamy kitchen. I loved to be the one to pop open a new jar and take in the scent.

After I enjoyed my sandwich, I changed clothes, put on sneakers and grabbed my library card. It was only three blocks to the public library where I could satisfy my nearly insatiable appetite for books. I usually had to go it alone, because my friends weren't as interested in books as I was. Colleen would only read teen idol magazines and, as far as I knew, Suzy didn't read anything, unless it was a school assignment. Even then she put up a fight. She was not exactly a model student, and in fact, had been left back in fourth grade. Now she was a grade behind me in school despite being several months older.

I wouldn't have minded walking the three blocks alone except for one thing, or should I say two things: the Marshall's dogs. The Marshall family lived catty corner to the library and they had the two hugest, meanest Irish Wolfhounds that were nearly as tall as I was. They were supposed to be chained up in the yard, but they often seemed to be running loose and would jump over the hedge when they saw me coming. I was terrified of these giants.

It is truly a testament to my love of reading that I braved the beasts every few days just to get new books. The library limit was four books at a time, and I could finish those in two or three days. On this particular day, the hounds were secured and could only bark at me as I walked up to the front of the library.

A Tudor style building housed the Spring Lake Public Library and a community center with a small theater. A large, spreading magnolia tree shaded the front entrance. I always admired the big pink flowers that bloomed in the spring. Its branches were low and heavy with large leathery leaves. Today I was surprised to see a girl sitting in the branches.

"Hi there" she said. I looked around, puzzled.

It was the strange girl I had seen this morning. Was she talking to me? And more importantly, why? I made a quick wave in her direction and entered the building.

The library smelled the way I thought a library should; slightly musty, with hints of leather and furniture polish. I had gone through most of the children's section of the library, having read all of Nancy Drew. I now had to suffice with the Hardy Boys. I didn't really like reading them; they all seemed the same to me, but there really wasn't much else to choose from. I picked a few of those along with a new Encyclopedia Brown the librarian pointed out, and I set off.

As I walked out the door I again heard a voice from the tree. "Did ya find anything good?" It was the girl in the magnolia tree.

"Huh?" I looked up and pointed to my chest "me?"

"Yes, you, silly bird. What did you get?" With that she leapt down from the branch and landed on the walkway in front of me. Astonished, I wordlessly held out the books for her to see.

Never had someone approached me in such a friendly manner. And certainly I had never seen anyone like this girl before. She wore cut off jean shorts that were fraying a bit around her tanned thighs. She had a halter top fashioned out of two red bandanas and wore several strands of colorful seed beads around her neck. Her hair and skin were dark but she had crystal blue eyes.

She looked at my books and smiled. "I read a bunch of these, too; I read kind of a lot."

"Yeah, me too." I looked down at my feet, suddenly afraid that I had been staring.

"Have you read Dinky Hocker?" She asked as she turned back toward the trunk of the tree and reached for a large blue denim bag that was bundled there. She rummaged through the sack, pulled out a worn paperback and handed it to me.

"*Dinky Hocker Shoots Smack*??" I read the title out loud. "Never heard of it"

"It's cool, you should read it some time."

"Yeah, I don't know. Maybe." My words failed me. Was this girl some kind of drug pusher or something? And what was with that bag she was carrying? It looked like it was made out of an old pair of blue jeans, with colorful embroidery all over it. It had a flap across the front with leather fringe hanging off.

"I'm Trish, what's your name?" She stuck out her hand.

"Uh, I'm Peggy." I clumsily shook her hand, something that the kids I knew just didn't do. Who was this strange creature and why on earth was she talking to me?

"What beach to you go to?" she asked.

"North Beach"

"By the pavilion?"

"No, that's North End. North Beach is further up."

"That doesn't make much sense, does it?" she smiled.

"I guess not." I had never thought about it before, but she was right.

"Well, Pegg-O, maybe I'll see you there." With that she ran off down the sidewalk in her bare feet. A pair of buffalo sandals were hanging from the leather strap of her bag, bouncing against her hip as she trotted out of sight. She must have been wearing perfume, because she left behind a heady scent, not like flowers or fruit, but more woodsy and mysterious. I sniffed the hand that she had shaken, trying to recapture the aroma. I stood there for a moment or two before I headed back up the street toward home. This time I ignored the Marshall's hounds as they barked at me.

The block I lived on was unusual in that all of the houses were almost the same, but it was not a new development. The houses had all been built by a lumber company that used to be at the end of the street by the railroad tracks. The lumber yard was long gone but the houses were all still owned by whoever was left of the lumber family. We each had a small yard, but between the houses was a big grassy area that we all simply called "the lot." It was sort of a common area that any of us could use. The Blankenship's house sat back to back with ours, with the lot in between.

In the lot was a long row of garages. They were dilapidated cinder block structures with shared walls and big heavy garage doors on the front. The doors didn't move smoothly in sections like the doors of today, they were behemoths with giant springs that required at least two kids to open. There were always a few empty garages that nobody used, so the neighborhood kids were free to turn them into club houses, art studios, theaters or whatever else struck our fancy. That particular summer we were mostly interested in stringing beads and making macramé plant hangers. My friends and I were well on our way to covering one interior with colorful knotted yarn.

"I met the strangest girl yesterday." I began to tell Suzy the next morning after we met up in the lot and were cutting across the street to meet Colleen.

"Who was it, Hepplewhite's daughter?" she mocked.

"Don't be a jerk, you know she doesn't have any kids," I said

"Duh, everyone knows that's why she's a crazy lady."

Colleen came up behind us. "Who's crazy?"

"Old Mrs. Hepplewhite." Suzy pointed her finger to her head and twirled it, the international sign for crazy.

Colleen joined in the action, "Yeah she belongs in the looney bin. You know she walks around all day like she's carrying a baby. It's 'cause her real baby died."

"Cut it out, you guys are so mean." I really

wanted to tell them about the mysterious Trish; and more importantly, I did not want to hear any more stories about my next door neighbor, who frankly, gave me the creeps.

The Hepplewhites lived next door to me. A narrow dirt road that led to the garages separated our house from theirs. I didn't see Mr. Hepplewhite very often, but he seemed nice and normal enough. He would always wave and smile when he was mowing the lawn on the weekends. His wife was the one the neighborhood kids whispered about. She was a tall thin woman who always wore a scarf over her head. It was true that she always walked as if she was carrying a baby in her arms. She hunched over with her arms folded, her head was tilted to the side as if she was cooing to an imaginary child.

What I suspected, but my friends did not, was that Mrs. Hepplewhite slept in her car. She had a big station wagon that was parked in the lane below my bedroom window. I never saw her drive the car, but one night I watched her carry a bundle of blankets and get in the vehicle. I really didn't want my friends to know I had a crazy person sleeping right outside my window, so I kept quiet about it. It was one thing to make up crazy stories about people we didn't know, but this was my next door neighbor. The scary part was that I was pretty sure the stories about her were true.

The sidewalk we walked along was barely

wide enough to walk three abreast, and in front of some houses there were bushes and hedges that made it even narrower. Often one of us had to move behind the other two. Too often, I was the one in back.

"I really did meet a new girl at the library yesterday" I insisted as I pushed ahead and wedged my shoulders between them.

"At the library?" Suzy mocked. "What kind of dork is she?"

"She's not a dork, she's really cool, and pretty, and her name is Trish."

"Trish, Trish, smells like fish." Suzy jumped up and down and shimmied her shoulders as she sang.

"Stop it Suz!" I was getting upset.

"Yeah Suz, let's hear all about Piggy's new imaginary friend," Colleen joined in the taunting.

"Forget about it, you two are such jerks." I started running ahead, tears stinging my eyes. They were supposed to be my friends, why were they so mean?

After another block I heard them run up behind me.

"C'mon Peggy, we're just kidding. You gotta learn to take a joke." I guessed this was Colleen's way of apologizing.

Finally we reached the beachfront. "Let's just go, it's so hot, I can't wait to get in the water," I said.

"And I can't wait to see Chris!" chimed Colleen.

With that Suzy wrapped her arms around herself and started making kissing noises and moans, “Oh Chris, I want to kiss you and touch your wiener. Eww, let's go under the boardwalk Oh! Oh!”

“What is your problem today Suzy?” scowled Colleen. “You haven't said a decent word all day.”

“Shove it!” With that Suzy jumped over the railing and down to the sand, once again neglecting to show her beach badge. I showed mine to the old guy at the first staircase and let Colleen make the longer walk up to Chris's station alone. I glanced at the old man's chalkboard.

You can discover what your enemy fears most by observing the means he uses to frighten you. Eric Hoffer

H2O Temp: 68 Low Tide 1:15

Eventually we all ended up out in the water. My mother always told me the salt water was healing. Today it was a balm for my hurt feelings.

CHAPTER 3

After a few hours we decided it was just too hot for the beach and began the walk back home. Although I had showered off at the beach, my feet were still sandy and my skin felt tight from the dried salt. We stopped along Third Avenue to get a soda. Third Avenue was the main drag with a four-block-long downtown area. There were small shops and restaurants and way too many real estate agencies. On that day we were mostly interested in the small convenience store that had some candy and a good selection of cold drinks. Most days we would journey further down to a much better sweet shop but we were hot and sticky and just wanted to make it quick.

We stopped for just a minute to talk to Evan, an older boy who was a fixture in town. Some of the kids called him retarded because he was kind of slow and went to a special school. He was real friendly and usually wandered around downtown talking to whoever would listen. He seemed harmless, so we were nice to him.

As we left the store and turned the corner to head home we nearly ran into her. There she was, in the flesh, Trish. Today her hair was loose around her shoulders. She wore a blue jean vest and the same cut off shorts.

She smiled, "Pegg-O, what's happening?"

"Hi Trish," I stammered, "How are you?"

"Cool-O! Who are your friends?"

"Oh yeah. Uh this is Suzy and Colleen," I managed awkward introductions and let the girls size each other up. I guess Trish met with their approval because the next thing I knew our new found friend had joined our little group and was walking back home with us. Trish paired with me and Suzy and Colleen followed behind. Again I noticed her perfume, I was about to ask her about it when she turned her head and asked brightly, "So what are you girls doing next?"

"I don't know" Colleen answered, "It's too hot outside, I'll probably go home and watch the soap operas." Colleen's house had air conditioning, so for her, it made sense to spend time indoors. My house would be stifling.

"Wanna go to the garages?" I offered.

"I could swear you said you wanna go to garages." Trish turned her entire body around and started walking backwards down the sidewalk in front of us. "What are you talking about?"

"We have these scary garages that we hang out in, they have dungeons underneath them where they used to torture people," Suzy said.

I was annoyed. "Cut it out, Suz! They're just these big old garages that nobody uses. It's kind of like our clubhouse."

Just then Trish tripped over the uneven sidewalk and nearly fell over backwards. I reached out to grab her by the shoulders. She leaned forward, and reached her arms around my body to catch her balance. We ended up in an awkward sort of hug. Trish tossed her head back, laughed and squeezed me tightly. I felt heat rise up though my body and neck. I knew my face was turning red.

"Careful Trish, watch where you're going," I scolded and gently pushed her away.

She let go of me and turned to walk forward. "That settles it," she announced, "We're going to the garages. And Colleen, you are coming with us; soap operas are for old ladies."

"Let's do beads," I suggested. "Trish, I can share my beads with you."

"No need, I have tons of 'em." She patted her giant bag.

When we arrived at our block Colleen and Suzy went home to clean up and Trish waited on my front porch while I did the same. As usual I squirted off with the hose before entering the house. I needed to take a shower, but for some reason I felt nervous taking my clothes off knowing that Trish was sitting right downstairs on the porch. Why was I suddenly feeling so shy? It wasn't like Trish was going to burst into the house and come look at me naked. I took a quick shower and dried off. I wiped the steam off the bathroom mirror with my towel and looked at my reflection. My light brown hair fell almost to my shoulders. It wasn't long and it wasn't short, it wasn't straight, yet it wasn't curly either. It was just sort of there. I ran a comb through it, doing my best to make it look like something. I pictured Trish's locks: long, dark, thick. Why couldn't I have hair like hers? Or eyes so blue? Mine were just brown. Everything about me looked just brown, even my skin had tanned to a dull brown color. I stared a minute longer and then started. What was I doing, standing there looking in the mirror, when Trish was waiting outside for me? At least, I hoped she was still there. What if she got bored and left? I quickly got dressed and ran downstairs, taking the steps two at a time. I stopped at the front door and held my breath, then stepped outside.

Trish was sitting on a metal chair reading a book. She looked up and smiled when she heard the screen door close.

"Wow, that was quick Pegg-O, I'm glad you're not one of those girls that spends forever in the bathroom." She closed up her book and tucked it into her bag. I noticed that she didn't mark the page by folding the corner back, or using a bookmark.

"Didn't you just lose your page? I mean, don't you have a bookmark or something?"

She smiled and shook her head, "Nuh uh, I just remember what page I was on. That's why they number the pages."

"Really? What page are you on?"

"69"

"I'll have to try that sometime." I was doubtful, but if Trish did it, I wanted to try too.

Trish burst out laughing. I was confused, what was so funny? She must have seen the puzzled look on my face, because she immediately stopped laughing.

"I'm sorry, I just thought of something

funny."

"What?"

"Oh, just the whole thing about the garages and the dungeons and everything. Suzy's pretty funny huh?"

"Yeah, she's a regular riot." I didn't think it was that funny, but I let it go.

We went around back and met Suzy by the garages. She was waiting for us to help her open the door. We managed to heave the giant door up on its frame. A dank, musty smell immediately wafted out, but we ignored it; the cement structure was cool and shady on such an unbearably hot day. It was worth a little stink to stay out of the heat. It was the perfect day to sit and work on our beading. We spread out an old sheet that we kept rolled up in the corner of the garage.

We each had our own little kit of colorful seed beads. They were sold in slim glass tubes, like tiny test tubes with corks to keep them from spilling. We strung them onto fishing line for long necklaces or elastic thread for stretchy bracelets. I was busy separating out my favorite colors and making a pattern of blues and greens for a new bracelet.

Trish opened up her giant satchel and began to dig through it. I couldn't help but wonder what was in her mysterious bag. She pulled out a fabric bundle, the corners tied together like a hobo's bindle. As she untied it, the sound of tinkling glass and tiny taps filled the air. There was a little avalanche of color as dozens of tubes of seed beads rolled out onto the printed paisley fabric.

Each one contained a different color bead. She must have had the entire rainbow; not just one shade of blue or green, but navy, royal blue, turquoise, mint green, dark green and other hues I had no names for. I felt a little embarrassed that I had offered to share my measly selection of beads with her.

I was puzzled when she pulled out a spool of wire and a tiny pair of pliers. She rolled out some thin wire and began work on an elaborate ring with rows and rows of beads forming a zig zag pattern. I watched intently as her hands worked, ignoring my own project.

After a time Colleen arrived, her straw pocketbook hanging over her arm. Trish looked up from her work, "Hey Coll, what took you so long?"

"I had to shower, and brush my hair and everything," she tossed her long hair over her shoulder for emphasis, then scrunched up her nose, "it stinks in here."

"Eh, it's just a little mildew, you'll get used it" I said "Look at Trish's ring." Trish held up the intricately patterned ring for Colleen to see.

"Holy Cow! How do you do that?"

"Here, cop a squat and I'll show you."

The three of us gathered around Trish as she showed us how to carefully weave the wire through the beads to make wide bands for rings and bracelets. I had been watching her for a while, so I caught on right away. I started a bracelet, but soon realized that I would need a lot more beads to complete it.

"I'm running out of colors, anyone want to

trade some reds and oranges? I have tons of those."

Trish tossed me two full tubes of turquoise and bright blue beads, "Here Peg-O, take these, I've got plenty."

"Really? Wow, thanks"

I glanced at Colleen. She had picked up the technique and was well on her way to making a brown, black and white ring.

"Someday, I'm gonna give this ring to Christopher."

"Oh brother," Suzy sounded totally frustrated. Somehow her wire was getting tangled and the beads were not lining up right. She tossed the knotted mess across the garage. It pinged against the cement wall and fell to the floor.

"Someday, I'm gonna give this ring to Christopher," she mimicked Colleen. "Someday, I'm gonna give this foot to your butt if you don't shut up about Christopher." She stood up and walked out of the building.

"What the heck is her problem?" Colleen asked.

"I think she's just mad because her ring got messed up." I replied, not even looking up from my project.

Trish set her things aside, jumped up and skipped out of the wide garage door. I watched her talking to Suzy. I couldn't hear what they were saying, but it didn't take long until they were both laughing. A few minutes later they came back in and sat down to their beads. Suzy abandoned the new technique and got to work on a long, multicolored single strand necklace.

I wondered what Trish had said to Suzy, but whatever it was, it returned the peace to our group, at least for a little while. By dinner time our legs and fingers were cramped, but we were so excited to have beautiful new jewelry.

CHAPTER 4

The horribly hot weather stayed around for a few days. There was not even a hint of ocean breeze to keep us cool. My mother put a small fan in our bedroom window to make it bearable for sleeping, but it was not enough. The little bit of cool air it provided was cancelled out by its loud motor.

I could hear Linda tossing and turning in the bed across from me. Finally she jumped up and turned off the fan,

"Ugh, I can't stand it anymore. I'm sleeping downstairs. You coming?"

"You think it's cooler down there?"

"Of course, dummy, hot air rises."

I grabbed my pillow and followed her downstairs only to find my mother already had the same idea. She was snoring gently, asleep on the couch. I realized that she had given us the only fan, so it was even hotter in her bedroom.

"Grab some cushions" Linda whispered and began to take the flowered cushions off of the living room chairs.

My mother stirred and opened her eyes. "What are you girls up to?"

"It's too hot" Linda whispered, "We're camping out on the front porch"

"Ok, but stay on the porch, and no shenanigans." She closed her eyes for just a moment and then sat up. "Wait, wrap those cushions in a sheet. You don't want them getting dirty."

I dutifully went back upstairs and grabbed the sheets off of our beds then quietly slipped out the front door and set up camp on the porch. Linda was right, it was a few degrees cooler. The air was still and the ocean smelled strong. It wasn't the usual clean, salty scent, but a heavier, fishy smell that hung in the air. When you live a quarter of a mile from the beach, the ocean is a constant presence. Some days we could hear the roar of the rough surf from our house. This night we only heard the fans and air conditioners from the neighbor's windows.

"Mr. Green caught two kids trying to steal gum from the counter today." Linda worked at an ice cream shop near the south end beach. "He chased them down the street until he grabbed one kid by the back of the shirt and brought him back in and threatened to call his parents."

"Who was it? Did he get in trouble?"

"Shh, not so loud," she scolded, then continued in a whisper, "I don't know, they were some dorky summer kids. They have to be stupid to try anything with old man Green, he doesn't miss a trick."

"Did he call their parents?"

"No, the kid started blubbering and gave the stuff back and promised never to set foot in the shop again, so he let 'em go."

"Wow, he was lucky. Mr. Green is kinda

scary." I rolled over and punched my pillow, trying to get comfortable on the makeshift bed.

"He's not scary; he's really a nice guy. He always pays me on time and lets me take home my tips every day." Linda defended her boss, "He just doesn't want stupid kids stealing his stuff. If you steal stuff, you deserve to get in trouble."

"Did you ever steal anything?" I asked.

"Are you kidding? Mom would kill us. It's not worth it. That's why I have a job."

Linda sat up and rested on her elbows, "Why? Have you ever shoplifted?"

"No way."

"You better not; I wouldn't put it past Suzy or Cindy either."

"What? What do you mean?"

"Nothin', never mind" With that she rolled onto her side and the conversation was finished. Eventually we both drifted off to sleep.

The next morning the old man's board read:

All things must change to something new, something strange.

Henry Wadsworth Longfellow

H2O Temp 71: Low Tide 2:00

This message I understood completely. There *was* something new and strange going on: Overnight the water had turned a nasty brownish color. Only a few either very brave or very dumb people were swimming in it. Colleen and I decided that it looked too gross, but nothing stopped Suzy.

"C'mon you big babies, you afraid of a little colored water?"

Usually her mocking would have worked and I would have joined whatever she was planning, but there was no way I was going into that ocean. Not only did it look wrong, it smelled wrong. The scent hanging in the air was a mixture of dead fish and moldy bread.

Suzy didn't stay in the water very long. When she came out, Colleen and I sat and waited on one of the concrete benches on the boardwalk as she rinsed off under the showers next to the steps. She took a much longer shower than usual. The crud seemed to be sticking to her skin.

We left the beach early that day and returned the next morning to find the water off limits. Both the old man's and Christopher's chalk boards read the same. No quotation, no tide times, no water temperature, just big block letters saying, "No Swimming-Red Tide." By then it really did look red. The usually white foam of the breakers was distinctively rust colored. The old man told us it was an algae bloom and that it might be dangerous to swim in it.

The red tide hung around for the next week. For us, there was really no point in going to the beach if we couldn't get in the water. Our daily routine had to change.

We would still meet up in the mornings, but

instead of the beach we would walk downtown. We'd stop and talk to Evan, who usually sat on a brick wall outside the drug store drinking soda and eating candy. We would tell stories about the Stripers and Moses Walker and any other people we might see along the way.

At the end of the four block downtown area sat the lake that our town was named for. It was surrounded by rolling green lawns and well kept patches of flowers. There were always lots of people around fishing, or feeding the ducks and swans or simply taking in the views. I had often heard the area described as "picturesque." Almost every Saturday you could find brides having their pictures taken near the one of the two wooden walking bridges that spanned the lake. We were mostly interested in the small park and playground area on the north side. It had tennis courts and some old playground equipment, a couple of swing sets and seesaws. There was a little path that led down to a small hidden cove by the water. It was a good place to sit and share secrets and watch the crowds without being seen.

Usually around mid-morning Trish would make an appearance. She always seemed to know where to find us. The strange thing was, we had no way to find her. She never told us where she lived or her phone number. She always managed to evade our personal questions and change the subject. Sometimes she would flat out ignore us by rifling through her bag looking for something. She usually managed to pull out something interesting enough to make us forget our questions.

So far, all I knew was that she was here for the summer, was probably staying at one of the inns by the beach, and she was the coolest, prettiest, most interesting girl I had ever met.

One afternoon we were sitting by the lake watching the swans when I asked her, "Trish, you always smell so good. What's that perfume you wear?"

"Sweet Earth," she said as she dug into her bag. "It's actually three different scents that I mix and match." She pulled out a small rectangular tan compact and handed it to me. I opened it up to find three little sections of a brown colored waxy substance. Each one was labeled with a different description. The scent was strong and familiar.

"Sandalwood, amberwood and patchouli," I read the label.

"I like the patchouli best, but I usually mix in one of the others." She reached over and dipped her finger into the wax and spread it on the inside of her wrists. Then she took a second dip into a different scent and rubbed it on the back of her neck. Then she rubbed her finger along the third scent and reached over and touched it behind my ear. I held my breath as she gently dabbed the scent behind my other ear and around to the back of my neck.

"That's Sandalwood for you, stirring and sultry," she laughed. I looked at the little compact as she read the words describing the scent. Her voice dropped an octave as she slowly said, "Stirring sultry incense perfume from the heartwood of the great sandalwood forests of

India."

I didn't know exactly what those words meant, but there was something very grown up about them. I looked at Trish and started to giggle. Soon she was reading all of the perfume descriptions in a low, husky voice like on a TV commercial and we were both laughing. She stuck her thumb into the perfume and rubbed the inside of my wrist and gently lifted my hand up to my face to smell it. It was strange to let someone else control my movement that way, but it felt nice. I trusted her.

She put the compact back into her sack and pulled out a leather bound book.

"What are you reading?" I asked.

"Not reading: writing. It's my journal." She flipped it open and turned to a blank page.

"What, like a diary?" I was curious.

"More than a diary. I write poems and stories and make drawings too." She flipped through the book and showed me page after page of writings and drawings all done in bright colors.

"Wow, that's really neat! Where did you find a blank book like that?"

"At the stationery store near my house."

I took the chance and asked, "Where exactly is your house?"

"You swear you won't tell anybody?" She cocked her head in the direction of Suzy and Colleen who were spinning around on the swings at the playground.

"No, I promise, I swear, but why can't anyone know?"

She pulled me close and whispered, "I'm

from Michigan."

I was puzzled, what was wrong with being from Michigan? Why would that be a secret?

She glanced at the girls to make sure they weren't paying attention, then she took a green pencil and wrote just five words in her book: I RAN AWAY FROM HOME.

I gasped and watched her quickly take the pencil and draw a box around the words. She colored it in and just like that, the words were gone. Gone from the page, but not from my mind.

"Whaddya mean, you ran away?" I whispered, lowering my voice even more on the last two words.

"Shhh, Pegg-O, you promised not to say anything," she scolded.

"I won't, I swear. But why did you do it? And how did you end up here, from Michigan? And what about your family?" I had about a thousand other questions to ask, but suddenly Trish hopped up and ran up the path to the swings.

"You girls getting dizzy or what?" She jumped on the open swing and started twirling in circles and laughing with Colleen and Suzy.

I was in no mood for the swings. First of all, I felt nauseated just watching them spin; secondly I felt like I had been punched in the gut. How could Trish make a confession like that and then refuse to tell me any details?

For the rest of the morning I tried to get Trish away from the others to find out more about her, but she managed to avoid being alone with me. I grew more and more upset until I just didn't want to be near any of them. Between Suzy's constant mocking of everyone and everything, and Colleen going on and on about Chris, I had enough and went home.

Cindy and Linda were lounging in the backyard when I arrived home.

"What's up Piggy? " asked my sister.

"Where are Suzy and Colleen?" Cindy chimed in. "And why do you smell like a hippie?"

"What are you talking about?" I scowled.

"You smell like that crappy incense the hippies sell at the flea market," Cindy continued.

"Shut up, and leave me alone, I don't care." I stormed into the house and up to my bedroom. What does Cindy know anyway? I liked Trish's perfume.

A few minutes later I heard the back door slam and my sister came in. "What's wrong? Did you get into fight with your friends?" She sounded almost concerned. She sat on the bed across from me and began brushing her long thick red hair.

"No, but I get sick of them sometimes. Colleen is too boy crazy and Suzy is just, well, you know."

"What happened to the new girl I saw you with? She seemed pretty cool."

"Yeah, Trish, she's cool. But, she's kinda strange."

"Is it that bag she carries with her? What's with that anyway?" She took her brush and began to try to get the knots out of my hair. Mine was shorter, thinner and a dull brown.

"I don't know, never mind." I wanted so badly to blurt out the secret, to tell my sister what I had learned, but I had promised; I had sworn not to tell. Besides, what was there to tell? I really didn't know anything. I allowed her to continue brushing my hair as tears slid down my cheeks.

"Ouch, stop pulling so hard!" I pretended it was all the tugging and pulling on my scalp causing the tears, but the pain was from somewhere else. She finished brushing in silence. This was one nice thing about my sister; she understood my need for quiet sometimes. We went to the kitchen, had our usual peanut butter and jelly sandwiches and Linda went back out to find Cindy, leaving me and my newly smoothed hair alone.

I sat on the porch and read until I finished my book. It was time for another trip to the library. I started off down the block and felt the familiar sense of dread rising in my stomach; I did not want to face the hounds today. I made a right turn and walked down the next street so that I could avoid them. This made me feel even worse, what a baby, walking two blocks out of my way because I was afraid of some stupid dogs, which might not even be loose!

I stormed into the library and looked for some books. I went back to the children's section where I usually found my mysteries, but realized I had already read every title there.

"Stupid library." I silently fumed, "they never get anything new. They only have little kids books and adult stuff. Nothing decent for someone like me."

In school we read *Jane Eyre* and some book by Jack London, but these bored me. They were old fashioned. I wanted stories about real kids my age. Why were all the books either for babies or kids who lived 100 years ago?

Then I saw it, on the cart next to the librarian's desk, a hardcover book designed to look like a brick wall, the title was in big yellow graffiti letters: *Dinky Hocker Shoots Smack* by ME Kerr. It was the book that Trish had talked about the first time we met. I picked it up and opened the stiff spine. I flipped to the back; it was brand new! There were no date stamps on the little envelope glued inside the back cover. I was the first one to borrow it. Things were looking up! I handed it to the librarian along with my card.

She raised her eyebrows, "Well, this is a little different than your usual read." She looked up at me, "but, I think you'll like it." She finished stamping the card and handed the book to me. She smiled over her half glasses, "enjoy."

Somehow I felt much better on the walk home. I had a brand new copy of a really cool book. I was probably the first one in town to read it, well, except for Trish and the librarian. Did librarians really read every book in the entire library? Who knows? Who cares? The important one is Trish. Now Trish and I will have something else in common, something special.

Just then I stopped in my tracks. The dogs were loose! In my excitement I had forgotten about them. They were just down the block, only a few houses away sniffing around in the bushes.

I hugged my book to my chest and began to walk, quietly forward. "Please don't come near me, please don't come near me" was my silent plea.

They both looked up. They saw me and started running toward me. Oh God, what should I do? Should I run away? Surely they would just chase me. I just stood there with my knees shaking. Can they really smell fear? The first one came up to me and began snarling at me. He was only a few feet away; I could smell his hot stinky dog breath. I could hardly breathe myself. Tears sprang to my eyes and I began to beg. "Go away, Go away," I sobbed, hardly able get the words out.

Then I heard a whistle. I looked across the street and saw a familiar figure coming up the block. He was incredibly tall, wore very short shorts and had a yellow beard; it was Moses Walker. He whistled again and slapped his leg. The dogs stopped and ran toward him. He didn't seem fearful at all. Next to him, the hounds didn't even look that big. Moses was not only tall, but he was big, not fat, but just large. I watched him pet the dogs and then shoo them on their way. They ran up the sidewalk and jumped back over the hedge into their yard. I just stood there holding my breath until they were back in their own yard. I looked up and saw Moses smiling at me.

"Thanks Mister." I managed to give him a little smile through my tears. He nodded his head and continued his giant strides down the street.

I realized that I was still gripping the book near my chest. I held on so tight that I left big damp palm prints on the cover. I wiped it off on my shorts and ran home as fast as I could. I spent the rest of the day with my new book. It was certainly better than anything I read before. Somehow the kids in it seemed more real, more complex than Nancy Drew and her pals.

CHAPTER 5

The next morning I woke early and could sense that something had changed. The hot heavy air that had been hanging around was replaced by a cooler ocean breeze. The air smelled fresh with just a hint of salt. I knew the red tide was gone.

I went downstairs and saw my mother scooping up a bunch of trash from the back step. "Eeew, Mom, what *is* that?" I scrunched up my nose.

"Just some garbage; now go back inside and mind your business." She quickly tossed it into the big metal cans by the driveway and wiped her hands on her apron. I did as she said, but still wondered how this trash came to be on our back step.

My mom was older than the mothers of my friends. Since my father died she worked sewing in a factory, but got laid off every summer. When the work picked up in the fall, they would call her back. This worked out well for her, giving her time in the summer to tend her garden, which was the envy of the neighbors. She never went to the beach, and didn't really like the water, but she encouraged Linda and me to learn to swim and was happy to see us spending time at the ocean.

On our way to the beach that morning Colleen suddenly said, “Quick, lets cross the street,” and started to cut across the road.

“Where you going?” called Suzy. Then we noticed Mrs. Hepplewhite coming up the block toward us. We followed Colleen across to the other sidewalk.

“Are you afraid of Mrs. Hepplewhite?” I asked.

“No,” Colleen insisted, “I'm not afraid, but my mother told me I should stay away from her.”

“Oh, so your mother's afraid of her,” cracked Suzy and then she began to tell us a joke. “So there's this boy and girl and their making out and stuff. So the boy keeps asking her to do stuff and the girl keeps saying no. So the boy says, 'Oh I love you so much, just let me put my finger in your bellybutton.' So the girl finally says 'yes' and he does it. Only the girl says 'Hey, that wasn't my bellybutton!' and the boy says, 'That wasn't my finger either'”

Colleen and I groaned, then Colleen asked, “Oh God Suzy, Where do you get this stuff?”

“My Uncle Chet told me that one. You get it? It wasn't his finger; it was his *you know what.*”

“Yeah, we got it,” I said, “I can't believe your Uncle tells you dirty jokes.”

By then we had reached the beach. All signs of the red tide were gone and all of the regulars were back in their usual places. The old guy's sign read:

To the soul there is hardly anything more healing than friendship.

Thomas Moore

Water temp 69: Hi Tide 3:15

We spread out our towels and ran down to the water which looked clear and beautiful. After spending a great deal of the day out in the waves we came back to relax on the sand. Small airplanes flew back and forth along the water line. Each time I heard the loud buzzing of the engine approaching I looked up to read the banners trailing behind the planes. The red and black lettering advertised local restaurants and bars. If you needed to know who was headlining at the Sea Girt Inn that night, you only had to wait for the right plane to fly by. We all sat up when an especially loud one with a sputtering engine announced *"You look burned, cool it with Noxema."*

"Let's play last straw," said Suzy as she began to build up a small mound of sand between our towels. I got up and looked around for a broken piece of beach grass from the nearby dunes. I stuck it into the top of the little hill and we had the supplies for our game.

The idea was to make up a challenge or dare; each person then had to scoop sand from the little hill. Whoever made the straw fall over had to complete the challenge.

Suzy made up the first dare. She stuck the straw into the top of the mound and spoke

"Loser has to walk right in front of the lifeguard stand and swing her bottom." The dares usually required you to do something embarrassing.

We took our turns scooping little bits of sand from the hill. I was ever so careful, because this was something I definitely did *not* want to do. Luck was on my side and the straw fell on Colleen's turn. She opened her pocketbook, brushed her hair and applied lip gloss before standing up.

"C'mon, just go." I was getting impatient.

"Hey, if I have to do this, I wanna look good!" She finally got up and sauntered over shaking her hips.

Suzy called out, "WooWoo, I wish I had a swing like that in my backyard." We erupted into giggles as Colleen stood right in front of the lifeguards and gave her long hair a toss and shook her bottom. She then ran back and fell onto her towel in laughter.

"OK, my turn to pick the dare." Colleen sat up and started rebuilding the hill. As she placed the straw in the top she declared, "Loser has to go up and talk to Christopher Flynn."

"Ugh" sighed Suzy, "You're the only one who wants to do that!"

We took our turns around the circle. I

noticed that Colleen seemed to be taking much larger scoops than usual. She really wanted to be the loser on this one. She took a particularly large handful and the straw started to go down, but then it stopped. It was leaning, but still hadn't fallen completely, and rules were rules.

My turn was next. I very gingerly touched the sand, trying to take the smallest scoop possible, but my luck ran out. The straw fell.

"You lose! Go catch a rap with Christopher!" Suzy taunted.

Colleen, on the other hand, was none too pleased. "Yeah, go catch a rap" She mimicked Suzy in a downright nasty voice.

This was a terrible situation; not only did I not want to talk to Christopher Flynn, I knew that Colleen desperately did.

"Why don't you go instead, Colleen," I offered.

"No Way!" Suzy protested, "You lost, you can't trade your dare!"

I stood and brushed the sand off of my bottom. I walked up to the boardwalk where Chris was sitting in his usual rocking chair, reading what appeared to be a comic book.

"Uh, excuse me, do you know what time it is?" I stammered.

"Time to buy a new watch," he looked up.

"Oh, that's so funny I forgot to laugh," I retorted. "Seriously man, can ya please just tell me what time it is?"

He put down his magazine and looked at his wristwatch. "It's 2:30"

"2:30? You better go to the dentist" I joked.

He looked at me like I had two heads. Did he really not get it?

"2:30" I repeated, "Tooth hurt-y, dentist, you get it?" Was he really that dumb? I swear I could see the light bulb go on above his head as he finally got the joke.

He began to laugh in a really loud and annoying way, "Tooth hurt-y," he snorted, "that's pretty funny." He sounded like a donkey.

"Yeah, thanks," I walked away, secure that I had more than fulfilled my challenge. What did Colleen see in this guy? I wondered. He's dumber than dirt.

As I was making my way back to the towels where my friends were sitting and laughing, I caught sight of Christopher's twin sisters, Kerry and Kelly, along with two others girls I didn't know. The Flynn twins were ultra popular and very snobbish. They both had strawberry blonde hair and freckles on their turned up noses. They always dressed alike. Today they had red and blue polka dotted one piece swimsuits and wore their hair in pig tails. I couldn't tell them apart, truthfully, I had never bothered to try.

"Who do you think you are Piggy Ryan?" One of them scowled at me. I didn't know or care which twin it was, nor did I know what she was talking about.

"What are you doing flirting with our brother? Do you really think he's gonna like someone like you?"

"I'm not." I stammered, "I don't like your stupid brother."

"We see you following him around and

making sure to go to his badge station. Everyone knows you have a crush on him." One of them was pointing her finger right at my chest.

"I swear, I don't care about your stupid brother, now leave me alone." I looked over at Suzy and Colleen to come and defend me. But instead of coming to my aid, they began to sing "Piggy and Christopher sitting in a tree, k-i-s-s-i-n-g..."

I was horrified. I could feel the heat rising in my body and was sure my face turned beet red. How could my best friends embarrass me like this, especially in front of the Flynn twins? Moses Walker was nicer to me than these two. He saved me from two nasty dogs, while my own best friends practically threw me to these two wolves.

"Stay away from Christopher, you ugly pig." The twin on the right sneered.

I turned and ran down to the water, sand flying around me. I didn't care if I kicked sand on other peoples' towels; I had to get away.

I dove into the surf and swam as far out as I could. I was swimming hard against the waves, huffing and puffing, tears stinging my eyes. Finally I rolled over and began to float on my back. I closed my eyes to the bright sun and let the water flow around my head, blocking out all sounds except for my own breathing. I didn't know or care how far from the shore I drifted. I just needed to get away.

I don't know how long I floated before I was aware of someone beside me.

"Hey Peg-O, I thought that was you." It was Trish; she seemed to appear out of nowhere.

I stood up and asked her "Where did you come from."

"I just got here and Suz and Coll said you were out here. What are you doin' out here all alone?"

I looked up into her beautiful eyes. Bluer than the sky, I thought, they sparkled like sapphires. I began to cry. "Oh Trish, why do they have to be so mean?"

I proceeded to tell her what happened with Chris and the twins and how my friends turned on me.

"Hey Peg-O, don't let them get to you. You know they only do it to get a reaction. Why can't you just ignore it?"

Why indeed? I wondered. It sounded so easy when Trish said it. But she was cool, and beautiful and smart. No one would treat her like this.

"C'mon, you're turning into a prune out here, let's go in." she said, "And don't worry, I've got an idea."

We returned to the towels and I lay down and avoided looking at Colleen and Suzy. Trish dug into her big bag, found a comb and combed out her long, dark hair. I watched as she held a colored pencil between her teeth and began to twist her hair down from the back of her neck. Halfway down she took the pencil and wrapped it right into her hair and stuck it through the bun. I was amazed how the smooth spiral stayed in place with just the help of a red pencil. She put her many strands of long beads around her neck, adjusted her bikini top, grabbed her bag and strode right up to the boardwalk where Chris was sitting.

"Where is *she* going?" asked Colleen.

I sat up to take a look. All three of us watched in awe as Trish confidently sauntered up and started talking to Christopher. We couldn't make out what she was saying, but she certainly had his attention. She hopped up and sat on the railing next to his chair. Then she reached out her long lean leg and put her foot right up on his knee. I don't know what he said, but it caused her to stretch her neck back and laugh. She looked completely beautiful and at ease. Chris couldn't stop staring, his mouth hanging open. Then again, neither could I.

I turned to glance at Colleen and she was turning colors. Her mouth was closed in a tight line and she was breathing heavily through flared nostrils. She looked like she might explode. I heard jealousy was supposed to be green, but Colleen looked absolutely purple.

Trish jumped down from the railing and grabbed her journal out of her ever present bag. Then she pulled the pencil from her crown; her hair tumbled down around her shoulders and she shook it just a bit. The effect was spellbinding. She used the pencil to write something on a page, ripped it out and handed it to Chris. Then she gave him a little wave and skipped away down the steps and back onto the sand.

We weren't the only ones watching. The twins were whispering back and forth as they watched Trish walk back along the sand. They clearly approved of her. Then they both put on their biggest, friendliest smiles and tried to get her attention. One of them beckoned her over with a wave of her hand. Trish smiled at them and then stopped and called to me, making certain that the twins could hear as well.

"Oh Peg-O thanks so much for introducing me to Chris. I'm so lucky to have a best friend like you."

I smiled and waved. The smile was absolutely real, I felt so relieved. How did she do it? In just a few minutes she had turned the entire situation around. Now the twins would know that I was not after their brother. Now they could leave me alone.

My relief was short lived as I heard Colleen mumbling behind me. "How could she?" she fumed, "She knows that I like Christopher. Your new friend is a real jerk Piggy." She practically spat the words at me.

"Me, what did I do? You're the ones who..." I was cut off mid sentence by the return of Trish.

"Hey Gals, guess who's playing tennis Thursday afternoon?" she said with a laugh and looked straight at Colleen. I was waiting for Colleen to jump down her throat, like she had with me; but to Trish, she didn't say a word.

Trish continued, "Col, you do play tennis, don't you? Well bring your racket to the courts by the lake at 3:00 day after tomorrow."

"What?" Colleen nearly did a flip "You mean, *I'm* playing tennis with Christopher?"

"Of course silly bird! I don't like tennis," then she lowered her voice and whispered to me, "And I certainly don't like Chris, he's dumb as an ox."

“Oh thank you Trish!” Colleen cried. “I can't believe I have a date with Christopher Flynn.”

“Oh brother,” Suzy chimed in “Now we're never gonna hear the end of this. Chris, Chris, Chris, Kiss, Kiss, Kiss.” Suzy continued making smooching noises until we were all laughing together.

Trish stood up and removed her beads, “Last one in is a rotten jellyfish!” With that, all four of us ran down to the water for the last swim of the day.

CHAPTER 6

Early the next morning I saw my mother cleaning more trash off of the back steps. Again she shooed me back into the house and told me to mind my own business. What was going on? Why was there garbage all over the steps each morning and why was Mom being so secretive? I went back up to our room to ask Linda, but she was still sound asleep. Lot of help she would be, she rarely woke up before nine o'clock in the summer, unless she had to work. I was determined to find out what was going on.

That evening I tried a trick I had read about, I drank four big glasses of water before going to bed. The idea was that my bladder would wake me up early in the morning without setting an alarm. As I climbed into bed I felt horrible with all that water sloshing around in my stomach, but I was sure it would work.

All night I dreamed about broken toilets, I kept looking and looking for a bathroom but they were always overflowing. Finally I woke up and realized the source of my bad dreams; I had to run to the bathroom in the middle of the night.

I didn't know what time it was, but it was nowhere near morning. Linda was softly snoring in the next bed. I peeked out the window down to the dirt road that ran between our house and the neighbors. There was the Hepplewhite's big station wagon, parked in its usual spot. Just a little bit of light from the streetlamp on the corner shined on it. I could just make out a large bundle in the back of the car. I stared for awhile and then for a split second I was sure I saw the bundle move. Was it a trick of the light, or my tired brain, or was Mrs. Hepplewhite actually sleeping in the car? I sat and peered out the window until my eyes began to close. I lay back in my bed and fell asleep. Not only had I missed my chance to solve the trash mystery, now I had a second question on my mind.

Colleen did not come to the beach with us the next day. We were pretty sure she was spending the entire day primping for her tennis match with Chris. I read the old man's board.

I've never known any trouble that an hour's reading did not assuage.

Charles De Secondat

H2O Temp 72 High Tide: 4:00

"Sausage? What the heck does that mean?" I blurted out. Then I looked at the board again and realized my mistake. I could feel my face turning red so I quickly ran down the steps away from anyone who might have heard me. At first glance I thought it said "sausage". What does reading for an hour have to do with sausage? What is "assuage"? I made a mental note to look it up in the dictionary when I got home.

Suzy and I had just gotten down onto the sand when Trish arrived. Rather than her usual blue jean shorts she was wearing bright white denim shorts that showed off her long tan legs. She had a single blue bandana wrapped around her top and tied in the center like a bandeau. Her hair was in one long thick braid down her back. Everything about her was perfect, even the way she carried her giant bag was effortless.

I really wanted to talk to Trish alone and my opportunity finally came when Suzy went up to the snack bar to get french fries. I moved myself over on my towel so that my head was right next to hers.

"Trish, I don't understand, where do you stay at night?" I whispered.

"Shh, I really shouldn't tell anyone, I shouldn't have even told you my secret"

"But I won't say a word; you know I'm not a blabbermouth."

She sighed, "OK, but this is the only time I'm talking about it. After this, we will never discuss it again." She took a long deep breath and began to tell a story.

"Both of my parents died in a car crash when I was eight. I was home with the babysitter and they went out to a party. On the way home they ran off a cliff."

"Oh, that's horrible. I'm so sorry. My dad died when I was eight too." I started to tell her but she cut me off and continued in a very quiet voice,

"I went to live with my uncle, but he is horrible. He gets drunk every night and sometimes he gets mad and hits me for no reason. I kept threatening to run away but he didn't believe me. He said I wouldn't get as far as the next town and I'd be back the very next day. Finally one day I did it. I took all my babysitting money and got on a train to New York."

I wanted to stop her and ask a million questions, but I knew this was my only chance. And Suzy would be back any minute. So I allowed her to continue.

"I tried to find my way around, but the city was too big and scary. I went back to the train station and saw these people on line buying tickets. They looked so happy with their beach bags and hats and one little kid had a rubber raft, so I got on line behind them. I bought the same ticket that they did and followed them to the train. When they got off, so did I, and that is how I ended up here."

"But where do you stay?"

"It turns out those people are only here on weekends. They have a little bungalow on Sixth Avenue. I sneak in and stay there during the week. I make sure to leave everything exactly how I found it, so no one even knows I was there."

She glanced across the sand, "Shh, here comes Suz-O"

I turned to watch Suzy approach us. She was walking with her towel all rolled up in front of her. When she got to us she allowed it to unroll onto our towels. Out tumbled a bunch of candy.

There was Turkish Taffy, two packs of gum, Razzles and even a couple of Slim Jims.

"Whoa", I said, sitting up, " I thought you were getting fries"

"Yeah, well this stuff looked so good. Here, have something." Suzy smiled and tossed me the Razzles, my favorites.

"I don't have any money," I figured she'd want me to pay her back.

"Don't worry about it" Suzy replied, "I hocked em."

"Huh?" I was puzzled by the expression.

"You know," she wiggled her fingers, "five finger discount."

"WHAT! You mean you *stole* them!" I exclaimed, lowering my voice on the last words.

"Yeah, I just stuck 'em inside my towel; nobody was looking. Don't be such a goodie goodie."

"You're crazy; don't you know how much trouble you can get in?" I looked at both Suzy and Trish, not even sure which one I was talking to. One was a runaway who snuck into strangers' homes, the other was a thief. I was no longer sure what to think of my friends; was I really too much of a goodie goodie? I tore open the stolen Razzles and popped them into my mouth.

CHAPTER 7

That night I had trouble falling asleep. I tossed and turned, my head full of questions. There were too many things happening too fast and I was unable to keep up. Colleen had gone on a date. She hadn't called to tell me what happened. I was afraid that she would be too grown up for me now. If she was dating Christopher Flynn did that mean she would start hanging out with his horrid twin sisters? The thought nearly made me ill.

Then I thought about Suzy and tried to pinpoint exactly what it was about her that made me want to be her friend. I remembered the first day I ever met her, nearly six years ago. We had just moved into the house when I saw her and her sister pushing each other up and down the dirt road in a beat up old baby carriage. They looked wild, with their tousled blonde hair, bare feet and dirty clothes. The carriage looked dangerous, and although they seemed to be having fun, I would have been scared to hop in. We became friends, I think, simply because of geography. Our houses were back to back separated by the lot. I wondered if I lived on a different block, would we have been friends? Suzy liked to tell dirty jokes and talk about sex. She did poorly in school and often got into trouble for breaking rules. I guess I shouldn't have been surprised at her stealing the candy, but it really bothered me. I was a good girl, wasn't I? Maybe I should stop hanging around with her before I got into trouble.

But what about Trish? Should I stay away from her too? She could be in a lot of trouble as well, she was actually living in a stranger's house without their knowledge. Was that theft? Breaking and entering? Could I get in trouble just for knowing about it? But how could I end our friendship? She was so beautiful and mysterious and easy to be around. She was funny and cool and had a special nickname for me. Besides, she seemed to be able to avoid trouble and solve any problem that came her way. And there was one more thing; she was always nice to me. She never mocked me or humiliated me like the others so often did. I just couldn't imagine not seeing her anymore.

I did not want to lose my friends, not Colleen, not Suzy and certainly not Trish. Tears streamed down face wetting my pillow. I laid there quietly sobbing until I drifted off.

When I opened my eyes, I could tell it was not quite morning, yet not still nighttime either. I thought of it as the grey time, just around dawn. My head was slightly achy from too much thinking and crying and not enough sleep. I looked out the window silently as Mrs. Hepplewhite emerged from the back of her station wagon in a cotton nightgown. She crawled out, sat on the back bumper and put a pair of slippers on her feet. She stood up and stretched then reached into the car, rolled a bundle of sheets and a pillow into her arms and quickly walk to the back door of her house.

I stared for several minutes trying to digest what I had just seen; my fears were correct. Crazy old Mrs. Hepplewhite slept in her car!

I sat and watched the sky brighten up, happy that morning had finally arrived. Mrs. Hepplewhite's back door opened again. She came out of the house, this time fully dressed with a colorful plaid scarf around her head. She was carrying a brown grocery bag in front of her, as if it contained something unpleasant. She walked past her car, across the dirt road toward our back yard. I saw her step onto our property, but couldn't see the back yard from my window. What was she doing? I snuck down the stairs to look out the back kitchen window. By the time I got there I saw Mrs. Hepplewhite returning to her house, empty brown bag in hand. I looked down at our back steps and saw what she had done. She had dumped a bagful of garbage on our stairs! It looked like a paper plate, some old orange peels and chicken bones, crumbled up tissues and some green stringy stuff I couldn't identify. I struggled with my feelings, I was angry that this crazy lady had thrown her garbage at my house, frightened at what else she might do and also glad that I had one mystery solved, one question answered.

I heard my mother coming down the stairs, “Good Morning sweetie.” She planted a kiss on my cheek, “You're up early.” She took the kettle off the stove and filled it with water. She returned it and lit the burner.

"Mom, what's going on with Mrs. Hepplewhite? She just dumped garbage on the back steps!"

My mother took a deep breath and slowly let it out while nodding her head. I knew she was deciding what to tell me. Finally she motioned for me to sit at the table and slowly began to speak, "Peggy, honey, Mrs. Hepplewhite is not right in the head. You see, she doesn't always know what she is doing. A long time ago she had a baby, a daughter. I guess she had fallen asleep one night with a cigarette burning and it started a fire. She and her husband were able to get out, but they couldn't reach the baby in the nursery. The little girl died in the fire. She lost her mind after that and they put her in the mental institute in Marlboro. But she refused to stay in the building at night, she kept escaping. So finally her husband brought her here to take care of her. She is still too afraid to sleep in the house, so she stays in the car at night, but I guess you knew that already."

She went to answer the whistling kettle and pour herself a cup of tea.

"Yeah" I answered, "I saw her get out of the car. Does she sleep out there even in the winter?"

"Yes, she runs the car for a while to warm it up and uses lots of blankets. I guess she stays warm enough." She sipped her tea.

"But what about the trash on the back step? Why does she do that?"

" I don't know honey, that's something new." She sighed and shook her head, "Maybe she sees that I have two beautiful daughters and she has none, so she is jealous or angry. I really don't know. Like I said, she is not right in the head"

"But can't you do anything about it?" I asked. "About the garbage, I mean. You shouldn't have to clean up her trash every day. Shouldn't you call the cops or something?"

Then I saw a side of my mother that I never suspected. She grabbed some paper towels and went out to the back steps to pick up the garbage. She scooped the nasty food scraps and used tissues in a ball. I expected her to drop it in our metal trash can, but instead she marched right across the dirt road and dumped the whole thing right on the Hepplewhite's back steps. She wiped her hands together and walked back into the house.

"Oh my God! Mom, I can't believe you just did that!"

She went to the sink to wash her hands.

"Well I'm tired of picking up her garbage. She has to know that she can't treat me that way. I really don't want to have to call the police, so I am hoping that she will get the message this way." My mother sat back down and continued drinking her tea. "Peggy, you can't let people take advantage of you. Sometimes you just need to stand up for yourself. Now, what would you like for breakfast?"

I knew the conversation was over and there was no point in asking any more questions. I sat down with a bowl of cereal while my mother started her daily crossword puzzle.

CHAPTER 8

I was curious to hear about Colleen's date with Christopher, so I met up with the girls and we sat on Colleen's front porch while she filled us in. It turns out that they were both pretty good at tennis, a game I knew very little about. Colleen recounted the scores of their matches, using the word "love" more than seemed necessary.

"Why don't you just say 'zero', why do you have to call it 'love'?" I asked. "And why is the score always love or 15 or 30? Why can't you just get one point for each score?"

"Don't be a dork, Peggy," Colleen answered, "that's just the way tennis is scored."

"Well, it seems dumb to me," I argued. "I like baseball, you cross home plate once, you get one run, simple as that."

Suzy jumped in, "Shut up about baseball, Piggy! I want to hear all about Colleen and Christopher. Did you kiss him? Did you let him touch your titties?"

"Oh my God, Suzy, you are so foul!"

"Shut up both of you," yelled Colleen. "Do you want to hear the story or not?"

"Okay, okay," Suzy said. "Tell us all about it"

Colleen went on with every detail about the date, what she wore, what he wore, how he took her to the ice cream shop after tennis and how they kissed goodbye.

"Wow! You DID kiss him. How was it?" Suzy asked.

Colleen gave a long sigh and smiled, hugging her arms to chest, "It was really great. We are going out again today after he finishes his shift at the beach."

"More tennis?" I asked.

"No, I'm going to his house. They have a built in pool."

A built in pool was something only a few rich people in town had. Even most rich people didn't bother since there was an entire ocean just a few blocks away. If they had money, they could join the fancy bath and tennis club that had a pool and a private beach. It figured that the evil Flynn twins would have something as unnecessary as an in-ground pool.

"So what are we waiting for? Let's go to the beach," said Suzy.

"I'm gonna skip it, I'm really tired, I didn't sleep much last night." I said my goodbyes and while they went down the beach I went home to finish reading my book. It was taking me longer to read Dinky Hocker than my usual books. Partly because it was a little more advanced, but mostly because I wanted to hang on every word and not miss any part of the adventures of Dinky and Natalia and Tucker.

I sat in a lounge chair in the back yard and read for awhile. I noticed that the trash had been cleaned up from the Hepplewhite's back stoop. I wondered whether Mrs. Hepplewhite had cleaned it, or if her husband had taken care of it. I wondered what would happen tomorrow morning. Eventually I dozed off and slept for a good part of the afternoon.

I woke up when I heard Suzy calling to me from the lot. Suzy and her sister Cindy were sitting on a blanket that they had spread out on the grass. I lazily walked over to see what they were doing. They had embroidery thread and needles but they were not embroidering fabric. In my sleepy state it took me a moment to register what was going on. They were sticking the needles into the bottom of their feet!

"What the heck are you doing" I shook my head.

"Check it out, the bottoms of our feet are so hard, we can't even feel it," Suzy said as she stuck the embroidery needle laced with green floss into her foot. "Look, I'm doing my initials."

I looked at Cindy. She had elaborate flowers embroidered on the calloused sole of her foot.

"Oh my God," I gasped "You two are crazy! Why are you doing this?"

"What's the matter, Piggy, don't you like it? I think it's pretty." Cindy wiggled her foot in my direction, the needle still hanging from it by a purple thread.

"Oh no, this is just too freaky for me!" I didn't really want to look, yet somehow felt compelled to stare. The truth was, Cindy had done a beautiful job on her flowers, they were colorful and intricate. But they were on her foot!

"I'm sorry, I gotta go." I ran back across the lot and in through my back door.

"Whoa, slow down Speedy Gonzalez." My mother caught me as I ran into the kitchen allowing the door to slam behind me. "What's your rush?"

"I think I'm gonna throw up." I ran upstairs to the bathroom, with Mom close behind.

I didn't throw up, but I felt a bit dizzy so I came back downstairs, plopped down on the couch and my mother brought me some ginger ale. "This will settle your stomach." I watched TV, some old cowboy movie that didn't really interest me, but it was the only thing on.

Linda came home from work a bit later "What's wrong with you squirt? Mom says you're sick"

"I'm not sick, just grossed out. The Blankenships were embroidering their feet."

"Embroidering feet? I don't get it."

"No, they were actually sticking needles and thread into the bottom of their feet."

" Eww, that's gross. Why?"

"I don't know. I guess their soles are so calloused that they don't feel pain."

"Calloused souls can't feel crewel pain," she mused.

"Huh?"

"Never mind." She slumped down in the easy chair. "Was Cindy really doing it too, or just Suzy?"

"No, they both had it. Cindy's foot was covered with flowers."

"That's just weird."

"Weird and gross." I offered, "How did they even think of doing such a weird thing?"

"Who knows? Sometimes Cindy and Suzy are just strange, that's all. How come you didn't join them?"

"C'mon, how dumb do you think I am?"

"I never said you were dumb. Sometimes I think you just do dumb things because your friends are doing them."

I lifted my leg up off the couch and shook my foot at her. "Well you don't see any embroidery on my foot do you?"

"I'm glad you had enough sense not to do it, that's all." She got out of the chair and walked up to the stairway.

I was pretty sure that was a compliment, so I let it go at that and closed my eyes as if I was falling asleep. The next thing I knew my mother was waking me.

"Peggy, it's nearly 9. You missed dinner, do you want something to eat?"

"No thanks. I think I'll just go to bed."

I went up to bed and thought back on my strange day. Mrs. Hepplewhite and my mother and the trash and Colleen and Chris kissing and Cindy and Suzy and their feet and Linda being nice to me. It all swam around in my head and got mixed up with TV cowboys and Tucker and Natalia, the characters in the book I was reading, and I fell asleep unsure of what was real and what was fiction.

I woke up the next morning feeling 100 times better and ran downstairs to see if Mrs. Hepplewhite had thrown her garbage on the steps again. My mother was sitting at the kitchen table with her tea and crossword puzzle.

"Well, you look better this morning, how do you feel?" she asked as she felt my forehead for a fever. "Are you going to the beach? It looks like it might rain this afternoon."

"I'm good, we'll probably just go for an hour or two," I replied, "Any garbage on the back step this morning?"

"No, I think she got the message. I doubt she will ever do it again." My mother was right, after that Mrs. Hepplewhite kept her garbage to herself.

I met up with Suzy and Colleen and we walked on our usual route to the beach. There was a stronger than usual breeze blowing. Even Colleen's perfectly coiffed hair was getting tangled. She finally gave up and tied it back into a ponytail.

I decided not to tell the girls about Mrs. Hepplewhite and the trash and the fact that she slept in her car. Besides, Colleen was too busy going on about Christopher and her afternoon at his house. Suzy was mostly interested in hearing about how they were making out on a lounge chair on the patio.

I was bored with the details so I asked, "Were the twins there?"

"Yeah, they showed me their room. They have about a million stuffed animals."

"That's queer," mocked Suzy

"Yeah, sort of," said Colleen, "Every time they go on a trip they get a new stuffed animal. Or if their parents go somewhere they bring them back. So they have two of everything."

Suzy couldn't resist, "Two of everything? Do they have two toilets in their bathroom so they can poop together too?"

"Suzy that is gross," I chuckled.

I looked up and saw Moses Walker striding toward us; his blonde hair shining in the sunlight. I hadn't seen him since he had saved me from the hounds.

"You feeling better today, hun?" He smiled at me and asked without breaking stride.

"Uh, yeah, thanks a lot," I replied with a smile.

When he was past us and out of earshot Colleen asked, "What the heck was that all about?"

"Eww, Did Moses just call you 'hun'?" said Suzy.

"No," I insisted.

"He did too" said Suzy, "He called you his honey"

"Stop it. He's just a nice man" I was getting a little whiny "He helped me the other day."

"So now he's your boyfriend." Suzy started chanting, "Piggy and Moses sitting in a tree"

Colleen joined in, "K-i-s-s-i-n-g, first comes love, then comes marriage, then comes Piggy with a baby carriage"

"Stop it you jerks," I yelled, "If it wasn't for him, the Marshall's dogs would have eaten me alive!"

"Really? What happened?" asked Colleen.

I told them the story of my run-in with the hounds and how Moses, or whatever his name was, called them off.

"Man, those dogs are evil," said Suzy

"Yep, the evil twins," I added.

"I'll bet their names are Kerry and Kelly"

"Oh God, you're right Suzy," I was laughing, "that's who they are, Kerry and Kelly the Irish Wolfhounds"

We all laughed about the dogs and soon enough we had reached the boardwalk. The old Man's black board read:

There are some things you learn best in calm, and some in storm. Willa Cather.

H2O temp: 69 Low tide 9:30

CHAPTER 9

When we got to our usual place on the sand, Trish was already there waiting for us. Suzy sat down and showed us the soles of her feet. The threads were now dirty and frayed from walking on them. She kept picking at them, trying to remove what was left of the hanging threads. I tried not to look because it was so gross. I was really hoping that this was the end of the whole foot embroidery thing.

Colleen had come to the beach with us but spent most of the morning up near the boardwalk talking to Christopher. I wondered what they talked about; it looked like she just spent most of her time staring at him while he looked at comic books.

Suzy asked us to go to the snack bar with her, but after the last time, I didn't want to take the chance.

"Do you want anything," she asked with a sly smile.

"NO, no please don't get me anything" I answered.

"Ok, jeez Peggy, don't be such a baby," she said as she walked away

I looked at Trish. "I'm not a baby, I just don't want to get caught stealing."

"I know, it's cool. Trish rolled over on her

towel so her head was right next to mine. "So Pegg-O, if you could change one thing about yourself, what would it be?"

"Oh God, I don't know, there's about a million things."

"Well, you have to start with just one."

"OK, I guess I would change my name. I hate the name Peggy and I hate that everyone calls me Piggy."

"Well that's easy to change. Isn't Peggy short for Margaret?"

"Yeah, isn't that stupid? It doesn't even make sense, how do you get Peggy from Margaret?"

"I don't know, but can't you be Margaret, or Margie?"

"Ugh," I said, "Margaret sounds like an old lady's name."

"How about Meg or Maggie?"

"Maggie sounds cool, but it rhymes with faggy."

"So what? Kids can find a rhyme for just about anything."

"I like the name Maggie, but I can't just suddenly tell everyone to stop calling me Peggy."

"Sure you can, Maggie," she smiled.

For one brief moment, it actually seemed possible; I thought that Trish could do anything. But as soon as Suzy returned I knew that I would be laughed at by my friends if I ever mentioned changing my name. I was glad to see Suzy come back empty handed.

"The guys at the snack bar were eyeing me like hawks, I couldn't hock anything." She sounded disappointed.

I changed the subject, “Hey we should go for a swim before it starts raining.”

“C'mon Col, were going out, you coming?” Suzy called over to invite Colleen to join us in the water.

“Uh, uh, I'm gonna stay here.” She shook her head and went back to chatting with Christopher.

Trish, Suzy and I played in the rough water, jumping over the waves or ducking under them to avoid being tumbled. Within a few minutes I saw Colleen entering the water; I jumped up and waved to get her attention. She saw me, but didn't wave back. Instead she turned and started swimming south toward a small knot of girls swimming together a little further down the beach. I could just make out two strawberry blonde heads bobbing up and down in the waves. Was Colleen really going over to swim with the Kerry and Kelly Flynn?

“Check out Colleen,” I said, nodding my head toward her direction.

“Ugh, is she really hanging out with the Flynn twins?” asked Suzy “They are such dorks.”

We all stopped to jump over the next big wave.

“I can't believe she’s dumping us for those snobs,” Suzy continued, “I'm going over there to tell her what a jerk she is.”

“Suzy, don't, please” I whined. I was mad, but didn't want to get into it with Colleen and the twins. But there was no stopping Suzy, she went swimming over toward Colleen's little group. I tried to follow, but the waves were getting rougher so I went in to the shore and walked along the sand to watch.

Trish followed me. As an outsider, she didn't really know about the cliques that formed during the school year. She didn't seem to care who was rich or poor or popular or cool. Once again I felt lucky to have her as a friend.

We stood on the sand and watched Suzy and Colleen yelling back and forth. The surf was rough and we couldn't hear what they were saying, but I could tell they did not look happy.

"Listen, Pegg-O, oops, Maggie, I gotta go," Trish said suddenly. "I can't get caught in the rain, I got everything I own in my bag and don't want it to get wet."

"But what are you gonna do all by yourself hiding in that bungalow all day?"

"You worry too much Maggie!" She reached over, gave me a hug and ran off.

I turned and watched her skip up to the towels and grab her bag. I followed her with my eyes until she was out of sight. I had a strange sort of feeling as I watched her, a little ache in my chest. How could I be happy and sad at the same time?

When I turned back to the sea it looked like Colleen was holding Suzy by the shoulders. They were moving up and down with the swells and it was hard to tell exactly what was happening. I could only get a glimpse of them between the waves, which were coming in fast. Was one of the twins pushing Suzy's head under the water?

I needed to find out what was going on so I started to wade into the surf. When entering rough surf, you have to time it just right so that you can get out past the breakers between sets of waves. If you get caught by a breaking wave you can get knocked down or worse. I waited until five big waves crashed at the shore. I looked further out and didn't see anything swelling so I made my move. I started to swim out to get to the deeper water, but I wasn't fast enough. A big wave was beginning to curl! I either had to get out past it before it broke or try to get into shore before it knocked me down.

I tried to swim faster, huffing and puffing, but I had no chance. The wave broke right over my head. I held my breath and ducked down. I felt the hard rush of water hit my head and tumble me under. The stinging salty water went up my nose, filling my head and giving me a moment of panic. My head was caught in the swirling surf. I wasn't sure which way was up. Is this what it feels like to drown? Will the lifeguards see me and come help? Next I felt the scraping and stinging of my shoulder hitting the sandy bottom. It was painful, but at least I now knew up from down. I righted myself and pushed my head above the water. I took a deep breath through my mouth and opened my eyes. I had my back to the sand and all I could see was a grey wall of water in front of my face. Another wave was about to break over me! I quickly took another deep breath in and held my nose to avoid taking in more water. I plunged down as hard as I could and tried to sit on the sandy bottom. The water again swirled around my head; I had the same split second of panic, but this time I stayed upright. When the wave passed I quickly jumped up and found my bearings.

I began to drag myself back into the shore, half crawling, half swimming until I could stand up and walk. Something didn't feel right. Was it the salt water filling my sinuses? The scrapes along my left shoulder and arm? No, it was my bikini top! It had slid up and was rolled up under my arms. My chest was completely uncovered! I turned back to the water and tried to duck down, but now it was only waste deep. I struggled to unroll the fabric and cover up my boobs. I glanced around, but no one seemed to be watching. I finished putting my top back into place and walked up and plopped down on the wet sand.

I was breathing heavily and a combination of salt water and snot was running out of my nose. My ears were clogged and my swimsuit bottoms were full of sand. My arm ached; I looked at the red rough scraped skin. I sat for a minute trying to catch my breath. I heard the lifeguard whistle blowing loudly behind me. I looked to see who he was calling. Was he looking at me? Did he see my top roll up? No. He was pointing out to the deeper water and whistling repeatedly. He was signaling to Suzy and Colleen who were fighting each other in the water. One of the Flynn twins had Suzy by the hair and was pulling her head backwards while Colleen was trying to get to her face, but Suzy was furiously kicking and keeping Colleen away.

I watched in horror as my two best friends were kicking and thrashing in the deep water. Part of me wanted to go out and help Suzy, because she was outnumbered, but I was exhausted and afraid. Besides, I didn't like fighting, not even the play around wrestling that some kids seemed to enjoy.

Finally Suzy managed to get free and start swimming away. She came up out of the water and plopped down right beside me. She lay back with her hands on her chest, breathing hard. "I'm gonna kill that ugly dog and her stupid friends too"

"God, Suzy, what happened out there? It looked like they were trying to drown you!" I was still shocked by the whole thing.

"I hate those girls, they are stuck up jerks." She sat up and spat. "A lotta help you were. I can't believe you didn't come over to help me"

"I tried," I explained, "But I got knocked over and couldn't make it; I almost drowned, myself."

I looked up and saw Colleen, Kerry, Kelly and their two friends walking toward us. They looked angry. So did the sky. Dark clouds rolling toward the shore. I knew this was bad news.

Suzy jumped up and stood with her hands on her hips, as if daring them to do something.

"You're an animal, Suzy Blankenship," one of the twins started in. "You're a ugly, dirty beast."

"Oh yeah, why don't you mind your own business, Kerry, you stuck up little jerk," Suzy yelled back. Somewhere in the back of my mind I was impressed that Suzy could tell Kerry and Kelly apart.

Kerry replied, "What are you jealous because

Colleen doesn't want to be friends with you and your piggy pal anymore?" She looked at me when she made the "piggy" comment. It was unnecessary; I knew she was talking about me. Now, like it or not, I was involved.

"Why don't you just leave us alone?" was my weak reply. I stood up and started to walk up the beach to get my towel. I just wanted to get away from the whole scene.

"Where you going, chicken?" It was the other twin, Kelly. I heard them yelling behind me, making chicken noises, but I just kept walking. I thought I heard the rumble of thunder in the distance.

I gathered up my towel and walked up to the boardwalk. By now most of the people had left the beach. I hadn't gotten a block from the beach before large raindrops began to fall. I wanted to run home, but my body ached and my lungs still burned from taking in water so I walked slowly with my head down.

I felt someone come running up behind me. I turned to see Suzy. "This isn't over, you know," she snarled and ran past me.

"Wait up!" I called to her. Just then lightening lit up the sky, followed directly by a loud clap of thunder. I was so startled that I let out a little scream.

"Oh grow up, Peggy," Suzy yelled back as she ran on ahead.

"Grow up," what was that supposed to mean? I wondered. Was it because I screamed? Suzy knew I wasn't really afraid of storms; we had spent many evenings on my front porch watching the thunder and lightning. Was it because I didn't want to fight? What is so grown up about fist fights? I walked the rest of the way home wishing that Trish was there to fix everything.

By the time I got home I was soaking wet.

"Whoa, you look like a drowned rat," Linda greeted me at the back door. "Don't bring your sandy wet stuff into our room."

I threw my towel and shorts over the clothesline, not that they would dry any time soon, but I didn't care. I went in and took a hot shower; the water stung the raw skin of my shoulder but it felt good to get all of the sand and salt from my body. I spent the rest of the rainy afternoon in front of the television.

It rained all through the night and the winds began to blow. The weathermen were talking about a storm, maybe even a hurricane that would hang around for the next few days. The gloomy skies suited my mood perfectly.

CHAPTER 10

The next day Linda was talking to Cindy on the phone. Cindy was planning to come over and play cards. Linda covered the mouthpiece with her hand and asked me, "Should I tell her to bring Suzy too?"

"Sure, I guess," I said without much enthusiasm. Would she even want to come? Was she still angry with me?

A few minutes later Cindy and Suzy were huddled under an umbrella knocking at our back door. I could tell that Suzy was still not over being angry because she didn't say much as we sat down to a game of rummy 500. But we played the long card game companionably with our sisters as the rainy morning dragged on.

It wasn't until after a few hours that Linda disturbed the shaky peace by asking, "So where's Colleen? I thought you were like the three musketeers."

Cindy laughed, "The three stooges is more like it."

I kept quiet; I really didn't want to get into it with Suzy. Honestly, I wasn't even sure what the whole thing was about.

Suzy looked up from her cards, "Colleen McMann is nothing but a stuck up jerk. Now that she's friends with the Flynns, she thinks she is too good for us. Just because she's dating Christopher."

"What? Are you serious?" asked Linda "She's going out with Chris Flynn?"

"Yeah," said Suzy with disgust, "she was making out with him and everything."

Cindy jumped in, "Ugh, Chris Flynn is just a big dope; he can't get any girls his own age so he's going out with a 13-year old. What a perv!"

"Yeah, he's a creep," Linda said, "No high school girls will go out with him after what he did to Karen Richardson."

"Why, what happened?" And "Who's Karen Richardson?" Suzy and I both chimed in.

Linda began the story, "Karen is a really smart girl in my class."

"Really smart, but really dorky" Cindy added.

"Anyway," Linda continued, "all of a sudden Chis started hanging around with her and finally asked her out. She was so happy because she'd never had a boyfriend and really didn't have many friends. I'm sure you know her brother, Evan, that retarded guy who hangs out downtown."

"Yeah," I said, "Everybody knows Evan. But don't call him retarded; it's mean."

"I'm not being mean; that's what it's called. Do you want to hear the story, or not?"

"Yeah, Shut up, Peggy. Let her finish" said Suzy.

Linda went on, "Ok, so, it turns out that Chris was gonna be kicked off the high school tennis team if he didn't get better grades, so he was dating Karen so she would help him with his homework. I guess she started doing the work for him, because all of a sudden he was gettin' good grades even though he was still dumb as an ox. Well, Karen caught him kissing another girl and figured out that he was just using her. She was heartbroken but she dumped him and told him she wouldn't do any more of his homework. So now he was stuck because he still needed a report for his English class, but she wouldn't do it. So one night he went and started throwing stones at her house."

Cindy picked up the story, "Chris says he was just throwing pebbles at her window to get her attention. Like he was being romantic or something. But he threw a big rock right through Evan's window. It broke the window and scared the crap out of poor Ev. Karen's parents called the cops and everything."

"Of course the Flynns are big shots in town, so they got him out of trouble, but he has to work all summer at the beach to pay for the damage."

Suzy jumped in, "Oh man, throwing rocks someone like Evan, that's just mean." I was surprised to see this side of her. "He doesn't do anything but hang around by the luncheonette and drink soda and say hello to everyone who walks by."

"Wow," I said, "Do you think Colleen knows about all this?"

"I doubt it," said Suzy, "She's such a goodie goodie. I don't think she'd go out with him if she knew."

"Shouldn't we tell her?" I asked

"No way, she treated us like crap yesterday."

"Yeah, so what happened with you guys anyway?" Linda wanted to know. I was a little surprised that she was taking interest in the stupid fights of 12 year olds, but it was a long boring day; we had to talk about something.

Suzy explained "Ever since Trish fixed her up with Christopher, Colleen's been acting all stuck up. She went to his house and was hanging out with him and his stupid sisters. Then yesterday at the beach she left us to swim with them. They started talking about us behind our backs and Colleen told Kerry and Kelly that Peggy called them ugly dogs.

"What!" I exclaimed, "I never called them ugly dogs!"

"You did too; you said the Marshall's dogs were Kerry and Kelly."

"Oh, God, I was just joking. Colleen laughed about it too."

Suzy continued, "I know, she's two-faced. Anyway, they all started mocking us out in the water and Colleen said something really nasty so I tried to hit her, and then they all ganged up on me. We got into this big fight in the ocean and I swear they tried to drown me."

"Where were you during all this?" Linda asked me.

"I was getting drowned on my own. I tried to go help, but I got tumbled by a big wave." I pulled down my sleeve and showed them the big red rash on my shoulder from hitting the sand.

"Wow, you really did wipe out. I thought you

were just being a baby." Suzy looked apologetically at me and at the nasty scrapes on my shoulder.

"Yeah, I know. I'm sorry I wasn't there to defend you." We dropped the subject and continued to play cards for the rest of the afternoon as the storm raged on outside.

CHAPTER 11

After three days of stormy weather I was bored of hanging around the house and decided to go out. It was still raining, but the winds had died down and it was no longer thundering and lightning. I wanted to go find out what Trish was doing. I felt bad that she was stuck in a bungalow all by herself, so I set off with my umbrella to find her. She had mentioned that she was hiding out in one of the bungalows on Sixth Avenue. I knew exactly where she was talking about.

When I was little we lived right around the corner from the bungalows; they were tucked in behind Sheehan's motel. At the end of the season my mother would help Mrs. Sheehan clean them out and get them ready for winter. I remember one year they pulled all of the old mattresses out of the cabins and piled them outside for the garbage men to pick up. The other neighborhood kids were jumping off the roof of the bungalow and landing on the pile of mattresses. It looked like fun, but I was too afraid to take part. As I walked through the rain up toward the highway I wondered how I would handle it today. Would I jump off the cabin roof? Would I still be afraid?

When I reached the bungalows I wasn't sure how to proceed. I hadn't actually thought about how I would find Trish; should I knock on doors, or peek in windows? She wasn't supposed to be here, so I couldn't very well ask the neighbors about her. The last thing I wanted was to have her get caught because of me.

The bungalows were small square one story buildings laid out along a dirt driveway. Large puddles had formed in the rutted road. The buildings had tiny covered front porches, barely big enough for a chair. They were white with green roofs and trim; they all looked like they needed to be painted. I could see from the street that most of the little houses seemed dark and empty. There were no cars in the driveways. Many of the summer people were only here on weekends, and if they were here this week, they had probably gone somewhere else to escape the gloomy weather. I walked up to the first cabin and knocked on the door. I felt brave about doing this only because I was pretty certain that nobody was home. But maybe Trish was in there with the lights off. I imagined her sitting and reading by flashlight, or drawing pictures in her journal. I knocked again, "Trish, are you in there?" But there was only silence. I looked around me to make sure no one was watching, but there was nobody in sight. I walked up to the next bungalow; there was an empty beer keg on the front porch. It didn't seem likely that the family with a little kid stayed here, but I knocked anyway and was answered with the same silence. I walked up the dirt driveway to check the other cabins, but didn't see anyone at all.

Just as I was heading up to the last few bungalows I heard the sounds of a car on the gravel drive. I turned around and saw an old black car bumping along. I jumped out of the way to avoid being splashed as it drove right through a big puddle. The driver parked next to the last little building, got out of the car and turned toward me. She had long wavy blond hair pulled back into a ponytail. Wearing blue jeans and an old yellow tee shirt, she looked to be in her 20's. Not old, but not a teenager either.

"Hi" she smiled at me. She had a very friendly open face; she looked like she probably smiled a lot. "What are you doing back here, hun?"

I stuttered, "Uh uh, I'm just looking for my friend."

"Oh, well, there's nobody else around here during the week days. They all go back to the city." She opened the trunk of the car and began to take out paper sacks full of groceries.

"Can you give me hand with these? Who's this friend you're looking for?"

She seemed pleasant enough so I approached the car and grabbed a bag from the trunk. I was still carrying my umbrella, so it was a little awkward, but I followed her up to the porch."Carl, can you get the door?" she called out.

The green screen door swung open and I was shocked to see a very tall man with a beard: Moses Walker! Today, instead of his usual short shorts, he was wearing long grey sweatpants. I was so surprised to see him that I forget my manners. I just stood and stared until he reached out his hands and I wordlessly handed him the grocery bag.

"Hi," he said as he took the bag "What are you doing over at this end of town?"

The woman put her bags down on the little kitchen table and called over her shoulder, "She's lookin' for her friend."

"Yeah, um, I thought she stayed around here, but I guess I'm wrong."

"Well, come on in out of the rain sweetie," the woman said. I realized that I was still standing in the open doorway. Part of me just wanted to run away, but the cabin was nice and dry and they seemed so friendly. Besides, maybe I could find out something new about Moses Walker, or Carl, I guess is his real name. I stepped over the threshold and let the door shut behind me.

"I'm Mary Kay and this is my boyfriend Carl."

"Hi, I'm Peggy. I was looking for this girl with long dark hair and uh," I let my sentence trail off. How could I possibly describe Trish? What words could possibly capture her beauty and her spirit?

"Honey, there aren't any girls your age in these bungalows. It's mostly crazy young bennies who come here to have parties on the weekend. They don't have any kids," Mary Kay explained. "Maybe she's staying at the motel"

"No, no," I said "not at the motel. She said bungalows."

"Well, I don't know what to tell ya, we are the only ones who stay here all week," she smiled at me. "You want a soda or something?"

She was unpacking the groceries and putting them in an old refrigerator. The tiny kitchen area was open to the main room, separated by a low counter. There was a little hallway off to the right that led to the bathroom and bedroom

"Sure, thanks," I said.

She held out a coke and root beer, one can in each hand, I grabbed the root beer. Then she passed me the can opener. "Thanks."

She got herself and her boyfriend cokes and went over and sat on the couch. Carl was quietly playing a guitar while watching a baseball game on a large color television.

I sat down in a wooden rocking chair. "What's the score?" I asked.

"Yankees are up 3 to 1 in the second." Carl looked at me "You a baseball fan?"

"I watch it sometimes." I didn't want to explain how I used to sit on my father's lap and watch games with him. How I could still feel the scratchiness of his face and smell his beer and cigars. Or how much I missed him. We hadn't watched much baseball in our house since he died.

I looked at Mary Kay, "You know your boyfriend saved my life the other day."

"What? You two know each other?"

"No, I just called off the Marshall's dogs. They got loose and were scaring the bejesus outta this lovely young lady." Carl laughed. "They're not really so bad, all bark and no bite."

"Oh Carl," Mary Kay spoke up, "Those are nasty hounds and you know it. You're only safe because you're a giant." We all laughed at her good natured kidding.

As we sat watching the game Carl continued to pluck the strings of the guitar. He wasn't really playing any recognizable song; he was just going up and down the scales and playing little riffs. It was hard for me not to watch his giant hands as they easily slid along the neck of the guitar. I was mesmerized by his quick and graceful fingering on the frets.

I caught myself staring and glanced around the room; there was something strange about the place. Like some of the furniture didn't quite fit. The walls were kind of a dingy grey color and the woodwork needed repainting. But the TV was big and bright and looked brand new. The couch was old and beat up, but the coffee table and the chair I was sitting in were beautiful. I ran my hand along the wooden armrest. The wood was satiny smooth with a beautiful light colored grain. The table had different colors of wood that gave it a striped appearance. It was unlike any furniture I had seen before. How did they have such beautiful furniture in such a dumpy little house? I decided it was best not to ask.

I looked more closely at Carl and decided he didn't resemble Moses at all. Sitting there playing his guitar, he appeared much younger than I had thought. His skin was smooth and tanned and his eyes were big and warm and light brown, almost golden. His long hair was hanging loose; he occasionally pushed it back behind his ear. He smiled easily and when I pictured him without the beard I thought he was kind of handsome. The thought suddenly made me feel very self conscious.

Had I been staring? Did he know that I thought he was cute? What was I doing? His girlfriend was sitting right there!

I quickly finished my root beer and waited for the end of the inning then got up to leave. Mary Kay offered me a ride home, but I decided I'd better walk. I was glad she didn't insist, because if my mother ever caught me riding in a stranger's car, I would be in big trouble.

"If you see my friend Trish will you tell her I was looking for her?"

"Sure Peggy," Mary Kay said, "I hope we'll see you again soon. Your welcome to stop by anytime."

"Don't let the hounds get ya," Carl laughed and winked at me as I was on my way out the door.

It was still misty so I put up my umbrella and headed down the gravel drive. Why did he have to wink at me? What was that supposed to mean? And why did it make me feel so, so squirmy? "Oh Carl," I thought as I heaved a big sigh, then caught myself. *What the heck was wrong with me? I was beginning to sound like Colleen and her constant sighing about Christopher! Oh my God! Is this what it feels like to be in love? No, No, No, this couldn't be. I just met the guy, besides, he has a girlfriend, a really cool one at that. Oh, and he's also a grown man, way too old for me. Most importantly, I don't want to be in love. I don't want to turn into one of those silly girls wiggling their hips and putting on lip gloss for the boys.* I tried to put Carl out of my mind and think about Trish, but this was even more confusing. It was one thing to have a crush on Carl, yes he was too old and certainly had no interest in me, but at least he's a guy. Trish is another girl. Suddenly my stomach didn't feel right. I started to feel nauseated, like I had been riding in the back seat of a car. I took deep breaths and kept walking. It was probably just the root beer, I thought. I shouldn't have gulped it down so fast.

Where was Trish, anyway? I hadn't seen her since she left the beach four days ago. She had to wait out the storm somewhere. Had she found another hiding place? Had she been found out and sent back to Michigan? Why hadn't she come to my house? Maybe I could have asked my Mom if she could sleep over. I walked back home through the drizzle wondering about Trish. I pictured her hiding in someone's shed, or sleeping in a car. Then I remembered Mrs. Hepplewhite sleeping in her car and how I hadn't known about it for all these years. What other strange things were going on around me that I didn't know about?

CHAPTER 12

When I got home I was surprised to see a note on the kitchen table in Linda's handwriting. “Call Colleen” it said. I ran upstairs to find Linda and ask her about it. She and Cindy were up in our bedroom. They were huddled next to each other with the telephone receiver up to their ears, giggling.

“Beat it, squirt,” said Linda when she saw me enter the room.“No, nothing just my dopey little sister,” she said into the phone.

“It's my room too, ya know,” I said. “Besides I have to change out of my wet clothes.” I went to my dresser and grabbed a pair of sweat pants and a long sleeve t-shirt, suddenly realizing that I was cold from being out in the wet.

As I started to undress, my sister threw a pillow across the room and hit me in the back “Get outta here,” she yelled. “Don't start taking your clothes off in front of everybody. What are you some kinda perv?”

“No, I'm cold, I need to change”

“Go change in the bathroom, weirdo,” Cindy joined in.

I took my stuff into the bathroom and dried off and changed into the warm clothes. I wasn't quite sure what the sudden need for privacy was all about. We had all changed clothes in front of each other for years, what was the big deal all of a sudden?

I still wanted to ask about the note to call Colleen, but clearly Linda was in no mood to talk to me, besides, she was tying up the phone line. I couldn't make the call even if I wanted to.

I went downstairs and turned on the TV to watch the rest of the baseball game.

When Linda and Cindy finally came downstairs, I asked, "When did Colleen call? What did she want?"

"I don't know, she called this morning when you were out," Linda answered, "Where the heck were you anyway?"

"I went for a walk and was hanging out at my friend's house" I said, "What did Colleen say?"

"Nothing, she just asked if you were here and then said to tell you to call her. What's the big deal?"

"It's just that we haven't talked since the fight at the beach. Did she sound mad?"

"No, she just sounded regular. Jeez, why don't you just call her and find out?" She was starting to sound annoyed.

"Ok, I'll call her when the game is over; it's the ninth inning anyway"

"What's with the baseball?" ask Cindy. "Since when do you watch the games?"

"I started watching it with Carl and wanted to see the end." As soon as it was out of my mouth, I knew it was a mistake. Why had I said *Carl*? Why hadn't I just said *Mary Kay*? I could feel my face turning red.

"Who's Carl?" They both nearly yelled.

"Carl and Mary Kay are just some people I met. They are staying at Sheehan's." I left out the part where they were staying in the bungalows behind Sheehan's and let them think I was at the motel.

"How did you meet these people, and what were you doing at the motel?" my sister asked.

"Ugh, it's a long story, I'll tell you later." I turned back to the TV to watch the last out. "Game's over, I guess I better see what Colleen wants."

I went to the kitchen to use the phone. I was a little nervous about making the call, but I took a deep breath and slowly dialed Colleen's number. I hated calling her house ever since her mother yelled at me last year. Colleen's father had been working the night shift and was home sleeping during the day. When I called and asked for Colleen her mother scolded me and said I should know better than to call, that I woke up her husband, and that Colleen went to the moon. I still don't know how I was supposed to know that he was sleeping. It wasn't like I called in the middle of the night. I also don't understand why he just didn't turn the ringer off if the bell bothered him so much. But I have rarely called her house since, preferring to quietly knock on her front door instead. I thought about all of this as the phone was ringing. Colleen's mother picked up.

"Hello," she said.

"Hi, Mrs. McMann, I am sorry to call, but Colleen left me a message to call her. I am returning her call; she asked me to call her back." I rambled on, trying to make it clear that this phone call was not my idea.

"It's OK, Peggy, she's right here. I know she has been waiting for you to call. Hold on dear." She was pleasant this time. I was past the first hurdle.

"Hello," Colleen got on the line.

"Hi Col, my sister said you called?" It was more of a question than a statement.

"Hi Peggy," she said brightly. "How do you like this rainy weather?"

"Yeah, pretty crappy." Did she really call to talk about the weather?

"Can you come to celebrate my birthday on Saturday? I'm not really having a party or anything, but my mom said I could invite you for pizza and ice cream cake."

Was it really her birthday already? Of course I knew her birthday was August 18, but was it really late August already? I always associated Colleen's birthday with the end of summer. Just as I associated mine with the beginning of school, just a few weeks later.

"Uh, sure, I can come. What time should I be there?"

"Hold on." She covered the phone with her hand, but I could still hear her call out. "Mom, what time should Peggy come on Saturday?" She got back on the line. "How about 5:00?"

"Sure, that sounds good. How many people are coming?" I was trying to find out who was gonna be there, but really didn't want to ask.

"Oh, probably just you and my cousins from

up north."

"What about Suzy?" I asked

"Uh, I don't know," she stammered. "My Mom said to keep it small. Please, can you not tell Suzy about it?"

"Yeah, OK. I guess. I'll see you on Saturday." We said our goodbyes and hung up.

So Suzy wasn't invited. I didn't really like the idea of going without her. But at least it sounded like the Flynn Twins and Christopher wouldn't be there either. I just hoped I could avoid letting Suzy know about the whole thing.

The next morning I woke up to see the sun shining. I breathed in the fresh salty air and dressed for the beach. I really wanted to get back to our regular routine: Suzy, Colleen and me walking to the beach together, telling crazy stories, meeting up with Trish. But I knew it would never be the same. Even if Colleen and Suzy could make up, I feared that Trish was gone forever.

I went out the back door and crossed over the lot and knocked on the Blankenship's back door. Suzy answered and within minutes was in her swimsuit and ready to go to the beach.

"Should we stop at Colleen's?" I asked.

"I'm sure she's much too busy with the Flynn twins to hang out with us." Suzy still sounded a little angry, or maybe even jealous.

When we walked by her house, Colleen was sitting in a big rocking chair on her front porch reading a magazine. She waved and we climbed up the steps to her porch.

"You coming to the beach?" I asked

"No, I can't. My Mom says I have to stay home."

"You grounded or something?" asked Suzy, who had more experience with being grounded than anyone.

"Well, not really; my Mom just doesn't want me hanging out at the beach."

"Really? Why?"

"I don't know," Colleen sighed, "It's a long story. She doesn't want me getting involved with Christopher. It's really stupid, forget about it." She looked sad, like she might cry.

"Well. OK, we'll see you later I guess," Suzy said and hopped down the steps three at a time.

I gave Colleen a little wave and mouthed, "See you on Saturday" and we headed toward the beach. I was glad that there seemed to be a truce between Suzy and Colleen. I hoped that the fighting was over.

Within a few minutes we saw the Stripers jog by. But something was odd, he was wearing his blue suit and she was wearing red. They weren't matching. When I pointed this out, Suzy started making up a story about how his red suit had gotten covered in blood when he hacked up his next door neighbors or some crazy thing, but my mind began to wander. I kept looking around hoping to see Carl walking up the sidewalk, but his large frame was nowhere in sight. I tried to recall the crazy stories we made up about him, back when he was Moses Walker, but I couldn't seem to remember them. I could now only picture his kind face and beautiful eyes and the way he laughed. Moses Walker was no longer. He was

Carl, the handsome man who saved me from the hounds and winked at me, and reawakened my love of baseball.

CHAPTER 13

I was excited to get back on the sand and out in the surf, but somehow it wasn't the same. Chris was at his usual spot at the badge check, but without Colleen, there was no reason to walk the extra distance down to his station. I went down the old man's stairs. His blackboard read:

All appears to change when we change

Henri Frederic Amiel.

Water temp 70 High Tide 9:45

The entire profile of the beach had changed. So much sand had been washed away in the storm that Suzy couldn't take her usual leap from the boardwalk; it was too high for a safe landing. We checked in with the old man and walked to down to the sand. The beach was much shorter than it was before. The lifeguard stand was pushed back and everyone seemed crowded together, even though we were in all in our usual positions. There was just less space than there had been.

The storm hadn't done any real damage to the boardwalks or pavilions, the beach had simply changed shape.

A wind from the west made the water clear and glassy. I tried to relax and float, but I kept looking up, hoping to spot Trish swimming toward me. But that day and the next went by and we saw no sign of her.

The evenings had cooled off and I asked my mother if we could bake some cookies. She was a great baker and made the most delicious giant chocolate chip cookies. We made a batch and the next morning I wrapped up a dozen in waxed paper and put them in a small paper lunch bag.

I took my package and walked west towards Sheehan's cottages. There was a cool breeze blowing and the sky was a cloudless dark blue. The scent of the ocean was very mild. It was still too early for autumn, but the air held the promise of crisp fall days to come. I turned left at the railroad crossing and decided to walk along the tracks. Suzy and I had often walked the tracks together, but I had never done it alone. I felt brave venturing along the railroad by myself. For a while I walked by placing one foot in front of the other, carefully balancing along the narrow silver rail, but this was slow going and I was excited to get to Carl's house, so I began hopping from one tie to the next. I was only slightly worried that a train would come; I knew I would have plenty of time to jump off the tracks and down to the cinder path that ran beside them. Once I passed the train station, it was only another block west to Sheehan's, I hopped off the tracks and headed up Sussex Avenue to the bungalows.

As I turned into the gravel driveway, I could see that the area was not nearly as dreary and deserted as last time I was there. There was a small group of people loading beach chairs, an umbrella and a cooler into their station wagon. It seemed strange to me that anyone would drive the six blocks to the beach, but then again, I didn't take chairs or umbrellas or any of that junk.

When I got near the last cabin I saw Carl standing outside with his head tilted back, staring up at something in the trees. As I approached him I suddenly felt nervous. They said to come back and visit, but were they just being polite? People say things all the time that they don't really mean. Well, it was too late to turn around now, besides I had already gone to the trouble of baking the cookies. I walked up and stood next to Carl, he was wearing his usual short gym shorts and a grey tee shirt. This was the closest I had ever been to him. He smelled good, but I couldn't place the scent, something outdoorsy, like the woods, but not exactly.

"What are you lookin' at?"

He glanced down and smiled, "Oh hey Peggy. I was looking at a red belly but he flew off so I was just admiring the trees." He put his head back and stared up at the trees. I did the same. "Isn't it great?" he continued. "Do you ever just put your head back and look at the trees, the sky, the birds?"

"Not usually," I said, my head still tilted back

as far as it would go.

"Every day, darlin'. You gotta do this every day." We stood in silence for awhile, heads back watching the green leaves blowing against the deep blue sky. It really was beautiful. Finally, Carl stepped back and put his head down. I smiled up at him and offered him the bag.

"I made you some cookies. I mean, for you and Mary Kay."

"Homemade cookies! Well alright!" He opened the back and stuck his nose in. "They smell like heaven. Let's go see how they taste."

I followed him up the tiny front steps to the bungalow. The screen door had holes in it that had been repaired with little pieces of screening. Despite the patchwork, a fly had managed to get through; it was buzzing around the living room as I entered.

Mary Kay was lounging on the couch reading a magazine. She lazily waved her hand in the air to swat away the fly.

Carl walked over and playfully grabbed her feet. "Hey babe, look who's here with homemade cookies."

Mary Kay sat up, "Hello Peggy, what's this I hear about cookies?"

"I made them for you, chocolate chip." I sat in the same chair as last time and Carl took his usual place as Mary Kay made room for him on the couch.

He handed a cookie to Mary Kay and offered one to me. "No, thanks, they're for you. I got more at home."

"C'mon Darlin' you gotta share the

experience with us...or wait a minute, are they poisoned or something?" He winked at me.

"OK, I'll have one, just to prove they're not poison." I leaned forward and took the cookie from his hand and we all sat down to enjoy them.

"Oh my God," said Mary Kay, as she took her first bite, "These are mind blowing! Did you make them yourself?"

"Yeah, well my Mom helped, it's her recipe."

"Oh Hun," Carl chimed in with a mouth full of cookie, "You gotta give us the recipe. It's not a secret, is it?"

"Of course not"

"Well" Mary Kay said, "some people don't like to share their recipes."

"Oh, no, my mother's not like that at all. I'll write it down for you and bring it next time."

They each ate a second cookie, I didn't need another, I was just happy that they were enjoying them so much.

Mary Kay, suddenly tired of shooing the fly, carefully rolled up her magazine and sat very still, waiting for the pesky insect to land. With one quick move she slammed to magazine down on the table, sending the fly to meet its maker.

Looking satisfied, she laid back down and stretched her legs onto Carl's lap. "So Miss Jane, did you find your birdie?" she said in a mocking tone.

"I did." Carl smiled, "A beautiful male red bellied woodpecker."

I must have looked puzzled because Mary Kay went on to explain, "Carl likes to watch birds, like Miss Jane on TV."

"I get it, the Beverly Hillbillies." I said. I had seen reruns of the show for years and was familiar with the old maid birdwatcher, Miss Hathaway.

I looked at Carl, "That's cool."

He smiled.

"Cool?" Mary Kay laughed, "Peggy, you are the only person on the planet who thinks bird watching is cool! It is the definition of not cool."

"Hey, watch it Babe, I think it's cool too."

"Oh my God, you are hopeless," Mary Kay said and picked up her magazine and began thumbing through the pages.

Carl reached to the table beside him and picked up a small blue book. "This here is the bird watcher's bible." He opened it and leafed through until he found the page he was looking for. He reached over and handed it to me with his thumb in the page. "Check it out, red bellied woodpecker. There's a pair of them in the trees behind the bungalow. I've been hearing them all summer."

The center of the book had lots of colored drawings of birds; I looked at the woodpecker and then leafed through the other color plates. "I never knew there were so many different birds."

"Yeah, most people see them every day but just don't pay attention."

I looked up from the book and smiled at him, "Mostly all I see are the sea gulls at the beach."

"Here, check it out." He pushed Mary Kay's legs from his lap so that he could stand up. He walked over and his knees cracked loudly as he squatted down right next to me. He took the book from my hands and found a page full of seabirds. "Look at all the different beach birds: herring gulls and laughing gulls and sandpipers and plovers. They are the best ones to start learning on, because they are big and easy to identify. Next time you're at the beach, take a closer look. Notice the shape, the color of the feathers and even of the beak and legs."

"Yeah, OK." I was trying to concentrate on the drawings, but all I could think of was Carl. He was so close, I could smell his woodsy scent, hear his breathing. I watched as his large hands deftly turned the pages, pointing out this bird and that.

Mary Kay piped up, "She's not gonna be lookin' at any birds on the beach, you dork. I'll bet she's much too busy watchin' the boys, right Peggy?"

"Uh uh," I stumbled, my mouth suddenly dry, "Not really."

Mary Kay took that to mean that I wasn't going to look at birds. What I really meant was that I wasn't looking at guys on the beach. Then I wondered if Carl ever went to the beach. I had never seen him there. I imagined that he was a great swimmer. I imagined him in his swim trunks diving into the waves. I suddenly was aware that he was still squatting right next to me. I could feel the heat rising up my chest and neck and into my face. Why did I have to blush so easily?

"Well, thanks for the bird lesson Carl," I stood up to leave.

"Well thank you for the cookies darlin'." He stood up and stretched to his full height. I wondered just how tall he was, but decided not to ask. “We'll enjoy the rest of 'em later.”

“Bye Peggy thanks,” Mary Kay said lazily from the couch.

Carl walked me out to the tiny front porch. I walked down the driveway for a bit and then turned and looked back. He was still standing there watching. I waved goodbye and began jogging down the drive.

CHAPTER 14

On Saturday morning Linda walked downtown with me to help me find a birthday gift for Colleen. The Blankenships had gone away for the weekend, so without her best friend Cindy around, my sister was being nice to me. Their absence also made it convenient for me, since I didn't have to hide Colleen's birthday party from Suzy. We looked in a few of the little boutiques, but I couldn't decide what to get for Colleen. We were too old for toys, she didn't read books, her ears weren't pierced, and I was having a hard time finding anything.

"Why don't we go to the record store?" asked Linda

"Sure, we can go to the record store, but Colleen doesn't really listen to music. Besides, this record store is too expensive."

"I know. I hope we can get a ride to Two Guys soon." Two Guys was a big discount store several towns away. They had the biggest selection and the cheapest prices for records.

We spent time looking at records, but not buying any. Finally we ended up in the stationery store where they sold greeting cards, and gift wrap and pens and paper. In the back they had a little display of sealing wax and the metal seals to press into it. The wax sticks were like small flat candles with little wicks. They came in all different colors. I picked out a beautiful swirly red one that I thought Colleen would like. Then I looked at the seals. They had all the letters of the alphabet and the signs of the zodiac. I chose the Leo the lion stamp to go with the wax. Then I picked out a small blue velvet pouch to hold them in. Colleen had a pen pal and also wrote letters to her Grandmother, so she could use it for those. It would appeal to her romantic side, she could seal her love letters with wax. I thought it was a great gift and hinted to Linda that my birthday was less than a month away.

After I found a birthday card and was waiting to pay I glanced under the counter and saw a small sign that read, *blank books.* There were several sizes of bound journals like the one Trish had. I picked up a medium sized book with a brown cover. It was tooled leather with a flower imprint on the front. I opened it and leafed through the empty blank pages remembering the bright, fun artwork in Trish's book. I flipped it over; the price tag was $6.00. This was more money than I had.

"Are you buying that?" asked Linda.

"No, I wish. It's beautiful, but too expensive."

"What do you want it for anyway?"

"I want a place to write and draw"

"Why don't you just buy a copy book, it's a lot cheaper?"

"I don't want a copy book, or a note book. I want this book. It's beautiful and special and I'm going to buy it someday."

"Jeez, ok, I was just asking. Don't you have babysitting money?"

"I do, but I was kinda saving it for new school clothes."

"Well, like you said, your birthday is in a few weeks." Linda smiled at me. The clerk wrapped up my packages and we headed home.

When I knocked on Colleen's door at 5:00 that afternoon her mother invited me in. "Welcome Peggy dear, Colleen and her cousins are in the parlor," she said as she pointed me to the little room to the right of the door. Mrs. McMann was the only person I knew who used words like "parlor" and "divan." At my house we had a living room and a couch.

Colleen and her two cousins were sitting and playing a game. Truthfully the two kids, Holly and Robby, were not really her cousins, and their mother and father were not her aunt and uncle. In the McMann family all of the parent's close friends were called Aunt and Uncle. This boy and girl were no more related to Colleen than I was. I had met Holly and Robby a few times over the years, but didn't know them well. They lived somewhere in northern New Jersey and came to visit on occasion.

They were gathered around a game of Trouble set out on the coffee table. Holly was sitting on an ottoman and Colleen and Robby were on the couch. Robby was 13, he was tall and thin with long straight black hair. He had dark eyes and pale skin and looked like he spent most of his time indoors. His sister was a few years younger and wore her dark hair in pig tails with big round red balls on the elastic bands. Although she was only 10, she was taller than I was. Both Robby and Holly were hunched over. Probably a habit they picked up from being taller than all of their friends.

After I said my hellos and wished Colleen a Happy Birthday, she motioned for me to sit next to her. She scrunched herself over so that she was sitting very close to Robby. She did this just as he was leaning forward to take his turn popping the little plastic dome in the center of the game board. As her thigh pressed right up against his, his entire body jerked and he knocked over the little bowl of pretzels that was sitting next to the game.

Robby jumped up. "Oh crap!" His pale face turned bright red as he bent over to pick up the pretzel sticks.

Colleen patted him on the back, "It's OK Robby," she cooed. "I'l clean them up" This only made things worse. He started shaking as he fumbled with the pretzel bowl. I was afraid he was going to drop it again.

I reached across the table and grabbed the little crystal bowl from his hand, "Why don't you go get some paper towels, Robby."

He grunted and scurried out of the room. I didn't mean to order him around, but I felt sorry for the kid.

"Isn't he the cutest?" Colleen whispered to me.

I just smiled and shrugged my shoulders. I guess Robby had replaced Christopher as the love of her life, at least for today. We finished cleaning up the pretzels and Mrs. McMann came in and called us into the dining room.

"You can finish your game later," she warbled. "It's time for supper"

We ate our pizza and ice cream cake. Ice cream cake was nice, but it wasn't a real birthday cake. My mother always made special cut up cakes for me and my sister. She had books with instructions on how to take a regular round or rectangular cake, cut it up, rearrange the pieces and make it look like something spectacular. Over the years she had made us cakes in the shape of horses and dogs and boats and penguins and any number of designs. The first time I went to a classmate's birthday party I was shocked that she had just a regular, every day, round cake. I didn't realize that other people didn't make special birthday cakes. I was still getting used to the fact that not everyone's Mom was as talented as mine.

While we ate, I watched Colleen flirt with Robby. She found excuses to touch him and spent a great deal of the time staring at him. I wondered how she could so quickly switch her affections from Christopher to Robby, but I didn't want to ask.

After the cake it was time for presents. Colleen unwrapped a cassette tape recorder that was a gift from Robby and Holly and their parents. Her own parents gave her a new tennis racket. I felt like my little gift would be a real let down after those, but she was very gracious and promised to use it. She told Robby that she would write him letters and seal them up so nobody else could read them. Again his face turned bright red, but this time he smiled at her. I began to think he was enjoying her attention.

Soon the adults sent us to the backyard to play. Robby and his sister picked up a soccer ball and started kicking it back and forth while Colleen and I sat on lawn chairs and watched. This was the first time I really had a chance to talk to her.

"So I guess you and Chris broke up," I said.

"My mother made me. She heard some stupid story about him and said I couldn't see him any longer. Anyway, I don't care."

"Yeah, I can see you really like Robby now. What will your mother think about that?"

"I think she's OK with it; his parents are like her best friends."

"So are you gonna come back to the beach with us? There's only a few weeks left."

"I don't know, is Suzy still mad at me?"

"No, I don't think so, as long as you're not hanging out with the Flynn twins anymore. You're not, are you?"

"No, they turned out to be jerks." She put her head down and looked sad. "As soon as I broke it off with Chris, they didn't want to hang out with me anymore. I guess they weren't really my friends"

I actually felt kind of sorry for her and decided to cheer her up. "Wait till you hear about my new friend Carl."

"Carl who?"

It occurred to me that I didn't know his last name. "Carl is the real name of Moses Walker. He has a really nice girlfriend named Mary Kay." I told her about how they lived in the Sheehan's bungalows and left out the part about how I was there looking for Trish. I felt a slight pang of sadness when I thought about her.

"Eww, they live in the bungalows? They must be really poor." Colleen scrunched up her face when she said this.

"I don't know, they have really nice furniture and a new TV. Who cares anyway?"

"My mother would care; she would kill me if I went to the bungalows."

"Ok." I said, "We don't have to go there, but please come back to the beach with Suzy and me on Monday."

"Alright, and what about Trish, Is she gonna meet us there?"

It was my turn to look sad, "Col, I haven't seen Trish since before the storm. I don't know where she is is." My eyes welled up with tears; I was trying not to cry but my voice was shaky. "I keep looking for her, but I can't find her anywhere."

Just then we heard Robby call out, "heads up!" as the soccer ball came flying toward us. Colleen caught it and held it close to her chest.

"You want it Robby, come and get it!" She got up and ran away holding the ball. Robby chased after her and they disappeared around the side of the house. Holly waited for a few minutes and then decided to go find out what was taking them so long. A few seconds later I heard her shriek and come running back.

"EWWW, Robby and Colleen are kissing." she screamed "I'm telling my mom."

"Holly, come over here." I called her back to chairs "Don't be a tattletale."

"Yeah squirt." It was Robby who came running back from the side of the house. "If you tell on me, I'll tell all your friends about how you're afraid to go in the basement alone. Better yet, I'll lock you in the basement if you tell!"

"Ok, Ok I won't tell," she said, "but you guys are so gross. Aren't they, Peggy?"

Robby must have forgotten that I was there because he suddenly looked at me and turned bright red. He turned around and walked back to the house, his little sister following behind.

Colleen emerged from the side yard and sat down next to me with a great sigh.

"Robby's a really good kisser, much better than Chris," she said as she ran her fingers through her hair. "That was the best birthday present ever."

I didn't know what to say, so I just smiled and let her go on about how cute and wonderful Robby was until Mrs. McMann came out.

"Your Cousins are leaving now, Colleen, come say goodbye and thank your Aunt and Uncle."

"I'd better go, too." I stood up to leave. "Happy Birthday Col, I'll see you on Monday. Thank you for inviting me Mrs. McMann." I walked back across the street to my house, wondering what Mrs. McMann would really think about the kissing cousins.

CHAPTER 15

"Why do ladies rub their eyes when the get up in the morning," asked Suzy when we were on our way to the beach Monday morning.

"I don't know, why?" was Colleen's response.

"Cause they don't have balls to scratch," Suzy laughed.

"Oh God, Suzy, don't tell me you got that one from your Uncle." I groaned "Why does he say stuff like that?"

"C'mon, admit it, it's funny" Suzy replied, "He told me a bunch of 'em yesterday."

"Oh, Suzy, please don't." Colleen begged. "I really can't take anymore of your Uncle's dirty jokes. Besides, I have to tell you about my new boyfriend."

"New boyfriend?" Suzy asked, "What happened to Chris?"

"We broke up, he turned out to be a jerk. Anyway, Robby is much cuter."

"Who the heck is Robby? Where'd you meet him?"

"He's her cousin" I said.

"Eww!" Suzy screamed. "That's so gross. My Uncle said that if you have sex with your cousin your babies will come out all deformed and stuff."

"Stop it! He's not really my cousin, besides

I'm not gonna marry him or anything."

Suzy and Colleen went back and forth for awhile, but I wasn't listening. I was watching a large figure walking up the street. Even from two blocks away I could recognize his long strides. I hadn't seen Carl since I had taken him the cookies.

"Hi Carl," I said brightly as we reached him.

"Hey Peggy, how ya doing? You gonna come by and watch the game later?"

"Uh, I don't know," I stammered, I could feel the heat rising in my cheeks.

"Well, we'll be there if you want to join us. And don't forget, you promised me the cookie recipe." He smiled and walked on.

"Ok, yeah I won't," I managed say after he was nearly past; my mouth was suddenly so dry it was hard to speak.

"Holy crap!" Suzy burst out when he was out of earshot. "What was that all about? You're friends with Moses Walker?"

"She went to his crappy bungalow and everything," Colleen jumped in. "Oh my God, look at you Peggy, you're blushing. You like him don't you?"

"No, I don't *like him* like him; he's just a nice guy. Besides he has a girlfriend, Mary Kay, she's really cool."

"Besides, he's about 50 years too old for you," Suzy said.

"He's not really that old, I think the beard just makes him look older." I tried to reason with her, "and his name isn't Moses, it's Carl."

"So, are you gonna go visit him later?" Suzy

asked.

"I don't know, why? You wanna come?"

"Of course, I gotta check this out," she replied and I agreed to take her to the bungalow.

The old guy's board read:

If you reveal your secrets to the wind, you should not blame the wind for revealing them to the trees.

Kahlil Gibran

Water Temp 75 High Tide 12:35

Once at the beach we managed to avoid Chris and his sisters, and spent the morning enjoying the surf. I tried not to keep looking around for Trish, but I couldn't help occasionally scanning the shoreline hoping to see her.

That afternoon, as promised, Suzy and I rode our bicycles over to the bungalows. As usual, Suzy wasn't wearing shoes. I always put on sneakers to ride, afraid of catching my foot in the chain or the spokes. As we pedaled up the gravel drive we saw three guys sitting on the tiny front porch of the second house. They had a speaker set up in the window blaring out music by The Doors. The beer keg was gone; they were drinking beer out of cans.

"Hey girls," one of them called to us.

I kept riding, but Suzy stopped. "Hi," she

said as she hopped off her bike.

I stopped and looked back and saw Suzy walk up onto the tiny front porch. What was she doing?

"Come on Suzy," I called to her.

"Go ahead, I'll catch up with you," she replied as she sat down on the step.

I shook my head and silently agreed with Jim Morrison, who was singing, *People are Strange.* I rode the rest of the way up the path to Carl and Mary Kay's bungalow, parked my bike behind the car and walked up to the front steps. The screen door was propped open and I could hear the sound a of guitar. Suddenly I felt nervous about being there. What would these two adults want with a kid like me? Maybe I should go back and get Suzy, she was the one who was so keen on visiting.

Just then Mary Kay looked out the door. Her hair was falling in loose blonde curls around her shoulders. She was wearing a bright orange and yellow sun dress that came almost down to the floor. She smiled brightly,

"Peggy, c'mon in. Carl said you might be dropping by."

I entered the little bungalow. Carl got up from his place on the couch, "How've you been, Peggy?" he said as he offered his hand. I reached out my hand and he shook it gently. His hand was about twice the size of mine, his skin felt rough and calloused, yet somehow warm and comforting. And oh he smelled so good. What was that? He walked to the little kitchen and opened the refrigerator.

"Root beer?" he said and handed me a can.

"Yeah, thanks." I took the soda and sat in the beautiful rocking chair. This time there was a small wooden table next to the chair. It was tall with curvy legs that reminded me of ocean waves. The wood was dyed or painted a bluish green color. I was certain it wasn't there the last two times. I wasn't sure whether I could put my soda down on it and I didn't see any coasters, so I held the cool can in my hands.

Carl returned to the couch and picked up his guitar. He played quietly in the background.

"Did you ever find your friend the other day?" Mary Kay asked.

"No, she seems to have disappeared from the face of the earth."

"Are you sure she said she lived *here*?"

"Well, uh, she said she was staying here sometimes." Suddenly, I felt the need to talk about Trish. I had promised her I wouldn't say anything, and so far I hadn't told a soul, not even my best friends. But somehow I felt safe talking to these two. I took a sip of my root beer and began to talk. I told them how Trish had run away from Michigan and how she followed the people from the train station and how she ended up sneaking into the bungalows. I told them how I hadn't seen her since before the storm.

While I was speaking Carl stopped playing his guitar and turned toward me to simply listen. When I finished the story I had tears in my eyes.

"Oh sweetie," Mary Kay said gently, "Do you think it's possible that your friend was making it up?"

"Why, why would she lie to me?" I was near to crying, but didn't want to embarrass myself, not in front of Carl.

"I don't know, sometimes people want to appear more interesting, or just enjoy making things up. Don't you ever make up stories?"

I smiled, remembering the crazy stories we told about the people we saw on the street and how Carl had been one of those people.

Mary Kay continued, "Think about it, if she was really a runaway, where did she get food and do laundry and stuff."

"I don't know, I guess she took it from the cabin, or bought it or whatever." I pictured Trish; she never appeared to be hungry or dirty. I remembered the different clothes she wore, the bright white shorts and the different bandana tops. Her hair always looked beautiful and clean. She always looked perfect to me. Suzy looked more like a runaway than Trish did. Suddenly I jumped up, remembering my friend.

"Suzy!" I cried out, "I forgot about Suzy! She came with me but stopped to talk to some guys at one of the other cabins."

I got up and ran out the door down the gravel driveway. I heard footsteps behind me and before I knew it, Carl was walking right next to me.

"She's probably up at 602," I heard Mary Kay call from just behind us. "Those guys were going to hang around this week." We came around the curve and saw one of the guys sitting on the front porch of what I now knew was bungalow #602. Suzy's bike was standing right in front of the cabin. The music was still blaring from inside, I recognized the song from Ten Years After.

"Where's the girl?" asked Mary Kay, pointing to the bicycle.

"Oh, hey," the guy on the porch slurred. "She's right inside, c'mon and have a beer."

"You better not have given her any beer." Carl didn't speak loudly, but there was a threat in his tone. He told me and Mary Kay to wait outside and strode right in through the front door.

We stood outside the door and listened.

We could hear only Carl's voice above the music, "Did you touch her?" he sounded stern. There were some muffled replies and then Suzy stumbled out the door with Carl holding his hands on her shoulders.

"Hey Peggy, there you are. You shoulda come in for the party." Suzy said in a sing song voice when she saw me. I had seen plenty of drunk people before, but was shocked to see Suzy that way.

"How much beer did you drink?" Carl asked her.

"Oh, just a couple a cans. Hey, Moses, where we goin' anyway?"

Oh God, I thought, please don't call him *Moses*. He can't find out that we called him that.

"Suzy, this is Carl and Mary Kay. We're going back to their house. I'll get your bike."

Suzy walked along with Carl and Mary Kay while I lifted the kickstand on her bicycle and rolled it along to their cabin and parked it beside mine.

We went inside and Suzy plopped herself down on the couch. She picked up Carl's guitar."Hey can you play *Smoke on the Water?*"

Carl quickly, but gently removed the guitar from her hands.

"Let's be careful with that Suzy." He took the guitar and walked into the back room to stash it away.

"Ok man, it's cool." Suzy looked around, "So what's goin' on here?"

"We're just talking and we were about to watch the ball game," I said.

"Oh, you should come meet my new friends, Paul and Matt and Craig. They are really cool. Paul is so cute."

Mary Kay sat on the couch next to her, "Sweetie, how old are you?"

"Old enough" Suzy laughed.

"She's 13," I said.

"Suzy, you're gonna get yourself in trouble hanging around guys like that. They're too old for you. What would your parents say if they saw you drinking?"

"They're cool, my Uncle gives me beer all the time. He said it's time for me to learn about stuff. He said I need to know how to please a man," she replied.

"Suzy, cut it out, you'd be grounded for a year, and you know it." I was getting sick of hearing about her Uncle. I was also starting to think that something about him wasn't right; he was downright creepy.

"Ok, let's calm down ladies." Carl returned from the other room. "I think we better sober you up and send you home."

"I'll make coffee," Mary Kay said as she walked into the little kitchen and pulled out a Mr. Coffee. I had never actually seen this new kind of percolator before, except on television. She brewed the coffee and handed a cup to Suzy.

"You want some too, Peggy?" she offered.

"Ugh, no thanks," I said. "I really don't like the taste of coffee."

"Just as well, it'll stunt your growth," said Carl.

"Then maybe you should drink some," I teased. He and Mary Kay laughed.

"Too late for that honey," Carl said with a wink.

Again I felt the heat rise in my face, why did he have to call me honey, and wink at me? Could everyone see me blushing?

Suddenly Carl jumped up, grabbed Suzy and practically carried her out the front door. While I was busy turning red, Suzy was turning green. They just made it out to the little porch when I heard the unmistakable sounds of barfing.

"I guess coffee was a bad idea," said Mary Kay as she went back to the kitchen and put a tea kettle on the little stove.

I went outside to check on my friend. She was sitting on the little front step with her head in her hands.

"Oh," she moaned, "I feel so gross." I sat with her for a little while. Carl got the hose from the side of the bungalow and began to spray the vomit from the front of the house.

I heard the tea kettle whistling from inside

and a moment later Mary Kay came out with another offering.

"Here you go sweetie. It's peppermint tea, it'll make you feel better." She handed Suzy the cup and Suzy began to sip the fragrant liquid.

"Smells good," I said.

"Would you like some Peggy?"

"Sure, thanks. I never had peppermint tea before."

She brought out two more cups, one for me and one for herself. We sat on the steps while Carl went back inside. I could hear the sweet sounds of the guitar as we relaxed with our tea.

"I can't believe that summer is almost over," Mary Kay sighed.

"Do you live here all year round?" I knew the bungalows weren't winterized, but I wondered where they lived during the winter.

"Oh, no" Mary Kay laughed. "We have a house down by the beach, but we like to rent it out in the summer and stay here."

I must have looked confused, because she continued, "Carl owns a big house down on First Avenue. He rents it out to some rich old people from the city for just two months in the summer and makes enough money to pay for all the taxes and utilities for the entire year. Plus it's really cheap to rent this dump and it's kind of fun staying here. It's real quiet during the week and on the weekends it's one big party."

"Carl owns his own house?" It surprised me that someone so young could own a house. My parents never owned a house, we rented our place. "Does he work, I mean, does he have a job?" I suddenly thought about the fact that he was always home during the day. Maybe he worked at night.

"Carl is an artist," she said. "He makes beautiful furniture and sells it in fancy galleries in the city."

"Oh! That furniture inside, he *made* that?"

"Yep."

"Wow! That is so cool. I have never seen anything like it. I mean, it's really beautiful."

"You'll have to come see the place when we move back in to the big house. His grandparents left it to him. There is a giant garage in the back that Carl has made into a workshop. He walks down there nearly every day."

Suzy put down her tea cup and tried to lay down on the tiny wooden step.

"C'mon Suzy, you can take a nap inside," Mary Kay said as she gently led her back into the house. Carl gave up his seat on the couch and Suzy plopped down. The three of us went back out and sat on the porch.

"Well, so much for watching the baseball game," I said.

"Not so fast!" Carl jumped up and ran back into the house. He returned a moment later with a small portable television. He ran an extension cord out the screen door and the three of us watched the game outdoors while Suzy slept it off on the couch.

After a few innings Carl turned to me, "Peggy, does your friend do this a lot? I mean does she go off with older guys and drink?"

"I don't know, she just likes to have fun.

She's a lot braver than I am."

"Honey, what she's doing is not brave. It's stupid, and dangerous. She is looking for the wrong kind of attention."

"I know, but everyone likes her, she's funny and friendly and not at all shy."

"Peggy, she's only 13. She's getting in way over her head with guys like that. She's gonna to get herself into trouble. Do you drink, too?"

"No, I mean, sometimes at home my Mom lets me have a drink, but not to get drunk or anything."

"Yeah, well that's different. Listen, I know Suzy's your friend, but I think you better be careful, she has a lot more problems than you know about."

"Huh?" I knew Suzy was a little wild, but I didn't understand what he meant.

"It's Ok hun, just be careful, stay as sweet as you are." He smiled at me. I turned back to watch the TV so he wouldn't see me blushing.

When the game was over, I woke up Suzy. She looked a lot better than she had before. I thanked Carl and Mary Kay for helping to take care of her, and especially for not calling her parents, or the cops. We got back on our bikes and rode off. We didn't talk at all on the ride home. I was angry that Suzy had been so stupid. I wished I had never taken her to Carl's house.

CHAPTER 16

It wasn't until I got home that I realized that I still had the cookie recipe in my back pocket. In all the commotion I had forgotten to give it to Carl. Well, I thought, at least now I have an excuse to go back.

That night at dinner my mother announced that she had been called back to work. She was expected in on Wednesday, so she arranged for us to go shopping for school clothes right away. My Aunt was picking us up in the morning and all four of us were going to Two Guys.

The next morning Linda and I climbed into the back of Aunt Joanie's Buick for the shopping trip. I couldn't remember the last time I had been in a car. I could go for weeks, even months, without riding in a car. This suited me just fine, as I was prone to motion sickness. Since my mother didn't drive, we were always at the mercy of others to drive us anywhere. If a neighbor, or my Aunt, would offer to take us somewhere my mom would jump at the chance, even if it was just to the supermarket. My excitement of leaving the confines of the town was always tempered with the fear of puking in somebody's car. I had to carry a brown paper grocery bag with me as I sat in the cavernous back seat. I guess no one had figured out that if they let me sit in the front where I could see out the windshield, I would be much less likely to throw up. My mother would always give me a stick of gum, Wrigley's Spearmint, to help "settle my stomach". I would obediently chew it, all the while feeling worse and worse. To this day I cannot stand the taste or smell of spearmint. Luckily, on this day I made it to the store without barfing.

Two Guys was an enormous discount store that sold just about anything you could think of. It wasn't the best place to shop for clothes; it didn't have anything fashionable, but it was fine for basic stuff. My mother said she would buy us the essentials there and that Linda and I could take the bus to Asbury Park another day to shop for nicer things like sweaters and cute tops. We wandered through racks and racks of clothing and then took our choices to the changing room to try them on.

Two Guys did not have individual try-on stalls like most stores; they had one giant changing room for everyone. I was not particularly shy about changing in front of other people, but I knew Linda hated this part of shopping there. My mother stood by the door of the changing room while Linda and I went in to try on our stuff.

When I came out, my mother and Aunt Joanie were talking to a lady who was standing by the changing room door trying to help a little girl of about eight who was trying on a dress. At the same time the lady was trying to keep one eye on a little boy who was running around through the racks. Every once in awhile she would call out, "Yoo-hoo Mikey come over here by Grandma."

My mother tended to strike up conversations with people in stores, I was never sure if she knew them or not, but she seemed to be on pretty friendly terms with this lady. I heard a little snippet of their exchange while I waited for Linda to finish trying on blue jeans.

"They're a handful," the lady was saying, "but I am lucky that their big sister helps out so much. I feel bad for her; she doesn't have much time for friends because she is always baby-sitting these two."

"I guess it was a good thing we had so much time off this summer." my mother responded. I guessed that they worked together.

"Yes, luckily I was able to send the little ones to camp during the day so Patty had some free time to go to the beach. It was nice to see her go out and have fun. She's around here somewhere, probably over looking at records."

While Linda and I went to look for socks, the adults finished their conversation. We picked out new socks and underwear and were heading over to the big check out area.

On our way to the registers I thought I saw a familiar silhouette emerging from the record department. I stopped in my tracks. No, it couldn't be. The lean tanned figure, the long dark braid down her back, and the big denim bag slung over her shoulder. I only saw her from behind, but there was no mistaking her, it was Trish. I tried to call out, but my voice caught in my throat.

The woman with the two kids was calling,

"Patty, c'mon, help me with your brother."

She turned around and walked toward them. As she turned, her eyes met mine. The beautiful crystals showed a brief look of surprise and then looked down in shame. She turned and took a few steps toward her family and then looked back at me and mouthed, "I'm sorry."

I stood there dumbstruck, my mouth hanging open. I wanted to run over to her but I couldn't move. I didn't know what I was feeling. I was so happy to see that Trish was alive and well yet I was angry and confused and sad and I didn't know what to think. I don't know how long I stood and stared, but eventually my sister brought me out of my stupor.

"Hey Peggy, what are you doing?" she called,. "Bring your stuff so Mom can pay for it."

I walked slowly to the checkout and dumped my things on the counter. I felt like I was in a trance; things were happening around me, the check-out clerk was chatting, the cash register was clanging but none of it made any sense. I just stood and stared. Linda shoved a shopping bag into my arms and commanded, "C'mon, what's with you? Let's go."

Back in the car on the way home, I finally found my voice, "Mom, who was that lady you were talking to?"

"That's Ida Dixon. We work together."

"Are those her kids?"

"Grandchildren. It's a very sad story; they're her son's kids. He died a few years ago and she was left to care for them"

"Where's their mother? Did she die too?"

"No, but once he passed away, she had a nervous breakdown and couldn't take care of them. She went back to where she came from, Michigan I think. So Ida and her husband have the three grandchildren, the two you saw and a teenage girl."

"Did you say Michigan? Is that where they lived?"

"I'm not certain, Peggy. Why are you so interested?"

"I don't know, I think maybe I've met the older girl. Where do they live?"

"She lives up in Ocean. Where would you have met the girl? Patty is her name."

"Uh, I'm not sure. I think she was at the beach." I don't know why I lied; I knew exactly where I had met her. I could remember everything about her, nearly every word she had ever spoken to me. I had relived them over and over again in my imagination.

"Well, Ida speaks very highly of her. Apparently she is very bright and does well in school. She helps out a great deal with her little brother and sister."

But she's a big fat liar, I wanted to say. I kept my mouth shut.

CHAPTER 17

I didn't see either Suzy or Colleen for the next few days. Linda and I were busy getting ready for school. We only had another week before we had to go back: Linda to high school and me to the eighth grade. We had to go through our school clothes and find out what no longer fit, which meant Linda gave me her hand me downs. We actually had fun together trying on outfits and making plans when nobody else was around to ruin things. We were planning to take the bus into Asbury Park to go shopping and I was looking forward to it.

The morning we were in our room getting ready for the shopping trip Linda said, "Cindy and Suzy are coming with us"

"What? Do they have to?" I whined.

"What's your problem? They're like our best friends."

"I know, but sometimes Suzy is just so stupid, she drives me crazy."

"God, Peggy, not everyone has to be as smart as you."

"That's not what I mean. She just does stupid stuff that I don't like. I'm not sure I want to be her friend anymore."

"You're not exactly Miss Popularity, you

know. You're not gonna have any friends if you can't keep Suzy. You know that Colleen's just gonna ditch you when she gets another boyfriend."

"I don't care," I whined, "I don't need friends like them."

"Fine, if you don't need friends you can go live like a hermit or something all by yourself."

"That's not what I mean. I just want friends who are normal and nice to me."

"Well then stop being such a dork all the time." With that Linda slammed the bedroom door and left me alone in the room.

She was right about one thing, I didn't have many friends. I really couldn't afford to lose the few that I had. Would Colleen really ditch me for a new boyfriend? I thought back to the way she acted with Chris and the Flynn twins; Linda was probably right about that too. Why was I so bad at making friends? Trish was the only new friend I had found on my own and thought was really cool, but she turned out to be a liar. Carl and Mary Kay were my friends, but I couldn't exactly hang out with them at school. I pictured a six foot tall man with long hair and a beard sitting at the school lunch table and started laughing. I bet nobody would call me "piggy" if Carl was nearby. I lay on the bed daydreaming about how cool it would be if Carl came to school with me. Linda came back in the room.

"You coming or not?"

"Yeah, I guess so." I got up and went to my dresser and put my money in the pocket of my shorts.

"C'mere and at least comb your hair or something." Linda grabbed her brush and began to brush through my messy locks. "OK, now you look better, let's go"

I followed her downstairs and out to the front porch where Suzy and Cindy were waiting for us. I was surprised to see Suzy carrying a large pocketbook. Her sister had one too, but that wasn't unusual, she was older. I had never seen Suzy carry a purse of any sort before; in fact, I had heard her mock Colleen's purse on several occasions. I was tempted to say something, but decided to try to keep the peace by keeping my mouth shut.

We walked downtown and caught the bus into Asbury Park. It cost 35 cents for the ride; we always made sure we had a dime and a quarter to drop into the little basket next to the driver. Some of the drivers got ornery if they had to give you change. I sat very still on the edge of the seat silently praying that I would not get sick and puke on the bus. I loved the idea of going places on the bus, but I hated the smelly diesel fumes and the rocking motion. I held onto the seat in front of me with both hands, looking straight ahead, trying to steady myself.

"How you doing there, Peggy," Linda asked after a few miles. She was used to my motion sickness and could probably tell from the way I was sitting that I was trying my best to be calm.

"So far, so good," I replied, not turning my head to look at her.

"Oh God, Peggy, you're not gonna barf are you?" Suzy must have suddenly realized what

Linda was asking about.

"I wouldn't talk if I were you, Suzy." I blurted out. Right away I knew I shouldn't have said it. I didn't want to explain to Linda and Cindy about how Suzy threw up from drinking beer.

I held my breath for a few seconds, hoping nobody would question it; luckily they all ignored it and our secret was safe. I made the 5 mile trip without nausea, and was happy to get off the bus and start shopping.

We began in the big department store on the corner. I knew that the stuff would be out of our price range, but Linda wanted to check out the newest fashions. Then we did our actual shopping in some of the cheaper stores down the block.

Later in the day we went into one of the five and tens. While Linda and Cindy looked at makeup, Suzy called me over to a big spinning rack of jewelry.

"Come here, Peggy. Look at all these cool earrings."

I walked over and stood on the other side of the display. "No, Peggy, stand over here." She grabbed my arm and pulled me next to her. "Look at these," she insisted and pointed to several pairs of earrings.

"They're cute, but cheap earrings make my skin turn green." I said and started to walk away. But Suzy grabbed me again and spoke to me through clenched teeth.

"Stay right there, stupid!" she whispered.

I was puzzled, but stood by her for several minutes while she spun through the rack looking at all the different earrings.

"Ok, let's get out of here," she said suddenly.

"I want to go find Linda, I think they are still over by the make-up."

"I'll meet you outside," Suzy said and made a beeline for the front door.

I wandered back to the cosmetic aisle and found my sister picking out eye shadow. "What happened to Suzy and Cindy?" Linda asked, looking around.

"Suzy said she'd meet us outside awhile ago, I guess Cindy left too." She finished her shopping, paid for her stuff and we went out front to look for our friends.

I was a little surprised that the girls weren't waiting right out front for us. What was their hurry? We walked up the block toward the rest of the larger stores. Perhaps they went into the other five and ten store, or the shoe store on the corner. We peered into the windows, but didn't see them.

On our visits to this small city, we generally stayed within the two block area of the shopping district along Cookman Avenue. We would only go as far west as the big Army Navy store that sold blue jeans along with all the military surplus gear. We would sometimes go east, to the arcades by the beach, but that was usually on a separate trip. A shopping trip was for just that, nobody wanted to lug shopping bags through the arcades.

We turned off the main drag onto the next street. There we spied Suzy and Cindy sitting together in a small alleyway between two office buildings. They were perched on a low brick wall that ran alongside one of the buildings. Their big purses were spread out in front of them and they were sorting through a bunch of stuff. As we walked closer I saw that they were tearing the tags off of several pieces of clothing. Then Suzy reached into her purse and pulled out a huge handful of jewelry: earrings, necklaces, bracelets, all still on the paper cards from the five and ten.

Suddenly Linda grabbed my hand, spun me around and started pulling me back down the street. "C'mon, we're leaving. Let's go back and wait for the next bus."

"What? Why?" I stopped walking.

She pulled me harder and gritted her teeth, "Now, let's go!" We quickly walked back to the bus stop at the main corner.

"What's the hurry, Lin, there's not another bus for 10 or 15 minutes."

"Peggy, trust me, you do not want to be around the Blankenships right now."

I looked up at her, "They stole all that stuff, didn't they?"

"Shh! Keep your mouth shut and pretend you don't know anything. Oh crap, here they come." Just then Cindy and Suzy came around the corner.

"You kiddos ready to leave?" Cindy called.

"Yeah, we're going," Linda answered flatly.

The four of us stood quietly and waited for the bus. We rode home in an uneasy silence. I was too upset about my friend's shoplifting to even think about motion sickness. It wasn't until we got off the bus that I realized how sick I felt. I had a sudden taste of salty liquid in my throat; I knew exactly what it meant. I walked just a few steps from the bus and turned to the street and barfed right there into the gutter.

"Ewww! You are so gross," cried Cindy and she and her sister ran away from me toward home. Linda stood next to me and waited until I was finished. She picked up the packages I had dropped on the ground.

"Here, I'll carry these. You OK to walk home?"

"Yeah, I'm fine. I'm sorry." I started to cry as we walked up the block toward our house.

"It's OK. It happens. It's not like you did it on purpose."

"I know, but why does it always have to happen to me?"

"Who knows. I guess everybody has some weak part. You just have a weak stomach. Could be worse, you could be blind or something."

"Yeah, or really stupid."

"Or have two heads," She poked me in the arm.

"They say two heads are better than one," I laughed.

"Not if you're puking from both of them!"

We got back to the house and I cleaned up and we laid out all of our new purchases on our beds. Linda held up a flowered print top.

"You know, Cindy will have one of these in every color. I had to work all summer to buy a few, and she just goes and steals whatever she wants."

"Did you know she was shoplifting?" I asked.

"No, did you know that Suzy was?"

"No. Well, I saw her steal candy at the beach,

but I never thought she would take clothes, and jewelry and stuff." I thought back on the day, all the signs were there: the big pocketbook, the way she ordered me around in Woolworth's. She must have been using me to hide from the store clerks. "Doesn't it bother you that they get away with it?"

"A little, but there's nothing I can do, I just mind my own business." She reached into our shared closet and pulled out some hangers and began to hang up her new clothes.

"But don't you think we should do something? Say something?"

"Like what, Peggy? You gonna go to the cops or something? Don't be stupid. Eventually they'll get caught. I just don't plan on being there when they do."

"But Cindy is your best friend. You're together all the time." I folded my new sweater and placed it into my dresser drawer.

"Not really. As soon as school starts I'll be too busy. I'm on the yearbook committee and I'm going out for basketball." She mimed a jump shot.

"Basketball? Really."

"Yep, we're starting a girls team and my English teacher is coaching. It sounds like fun."

She was trying to change the subject, but I couldn't let it go."Well, I never want to go shopping with Suzy again. I still can't believe she stole all that stuff, all those earrings!"

"Eh, it's a bunch of cheap junk anyway. Do you really want crappy five and ten earrings? Don't they just turn your skin green?"

"Yeah, I guess."

"So don't worry about it, Peggy. Just mind

your own business. Besides, you probably won't see Suzy much in school either. The sixth grade is downstairs in the old wing."

"Sixth grade? Suzy's going into seventh and I'm in eighth."

Linda stopped fussing with the clothes and stared at me. "Didn't Suzy tell you?" she asked slowly.

"Tell me what?"

"Suzy's being left back. She has to repeat the sixth grade."

"Are you serious?" I sat down on the bed.

"Yeah, Cindy told me. Suzy failed grade six and has to stay back and do it again. They were gonna send her to some special school." Linda closed the closet door and sat on the bed next to me.

"What are you talking about? What special school?"

"You know, for kids who are dumb, or in trouble."

"Reform school?"

"No, not that bad. It's the same school Evan goes to."

"Evan? They wanna put Suzy in a *retard* school?" I dropped my voice to a whisper on the ugly word.

"No, it's just a school where the kids get lots of extra help. Anyway, she's not going. I probably shouldn't have told you. Don't say anything to Suzy. She's probably embarrassed."

Suzy, embarrassed? I thought. I had never seen Suzy embarrassed about anything. She would just make it into a joke. Everything was a big joke to Suzy.

Linda continued, "Cindy said that Suzy was really upset and didn't want to go to the other school. She cried and begged and promised to study if they let her stay at Mountz. They're gonna let her try it for the first marking period, but if she doesn't pass, she has to go."

"Oh my God! That's terrible. Shouldn't I try to help her or something?"

"If the teachers can't get her to do her work, how do you think you're gonna help her?" She shook her head.

"I don't know, maybe we could study together or something."

"Yeah, good luck with that," She said as she walked away, taking the empty shopping bags with her.

CHAPTER 18

I was still angry at Suzy for shoplifting, but I felt kind of sorry for her at the same time. I had an idea. I checked the time and found I still had 40 minutes until the library closed. I grabbed my card and quickly jumped down the stairs taking two steps at a time.

"I'm going to the library, be right back," I called out to Linda as I ran out the front door and down the sidewalk. The Marshall's hounds were nowhere in sight as I jogged by. I stopped for just a second before opening the library door. I glanced up at the magnolia tree. Would I ever be able to look at it the same way?

The library was empty as far as I could tell. Rather than going to the children's section or the card catalog, I approached the librarian, who was sitting behind her desk sorting through a pile of papers. She looked up at me over her glasses and smiled.

"Hi," I whispered "Can you help me to find something?"

"Of course, dear, what do you need?" She looked a bit puzzled. She must have known that I didn't need help with the Dewey decimal system.

"I have this friend, and uh, she likes weird and creepy kinds of stories, can you help me find something?"

"Horror stories. We have a whole section of them upstairs" She pointed up to the walkway that ran along the perimeter of the room. An iron stairway led up to the open catwalk. I had only been up there a few times. "Of course you can look in the card catalog under the subject."

"Um, I'm not sure that my friend can read that good. I mean, she doesn't really read books. I'm trying to help find something she might like."

"She doesn't read well." She corrected my grammar and continued, "Is she your age? What grade is she in?"

"Yes, she's my age, but she is in sixth grade. She stayed back. I thought that maybe if I found some really gross stories, she would try to read them."

"Really gross stories, you say. Hmm." She sat back in her chair, closed her eyes and put her hand up to her face and tapped her nose rhythmically. Suddenly she opened her eyes and whispered, "I don't have anything like that here, but how about the pulp magazines? The articles are short enough, so your friends won't get bored, and they are definitely on the macabre side."

"Macabre?"

"Creepy, bizarre. You'll have to go to the newsstand to find them; they have names like True Crime and Detective Story. They aren't exactly great literature, but if it gets your friend to read..."

"Yeah, I guess."

"Well good luck, dear."

I left the library and headed into town. A

woman in a brightly flowered dress and ruffled apron was outside the candy shop using a long metal pole to roll up the striped awning that shaded her storefront window. I realized it was nearly 5 o clock and the shop keepers were getting ready to close. I ran down the block and into the newspaper store. The little bell above the door jingled as I entered. The store had an old fashioned feel about it. The wooden floor was uneven and squeaky and the shelves were packed with newspapers and magazines. The sweet scent of pipe tobacco permeated the air. Behind the counter were glass cases with cigars and round tins of tobacco. Two elderly gentlemen were sitting behind the counter. I hoped I wasn't too late. When one of the old men looked up at me I was sure he was going to tell me that the store was closing, but he simply asked "Can I help you young lady?"

"Uh, yeah, I'm looking for magazines. I think they're called True Crime or True Detective or something"

"You want pulp. Right around the back there, third shelf 'bout half way down." He pointed to the back of the large wooden magazine rack the ran nearly the length of the shop.

"Thanks. Are you about to close?"

"Can't very well close when I got a customer, now can I?"

"Thanks." I walked behind the rack and stopped half way down the aisle. I had never looked at the back side of the magazine shelves. The front side displayed all the popular stuff like *Time* and *Life* and *Good Housekeeping*. Of course they had *Teen* and *Seventeen* and the fan club mags that Colleen liked, but the back of the rack was full of all sorts of stuff I never knew existed. There were magazines about cars and motorcycles, pets and horses and who knows what else.

I found what the librarian and the old man had referred to as "pulp". I paged through *True Crime, Weird Tales, Terror Tales, True Confessions* and *True Story*. Some of them looked like comic books, other were wordier. I didn't think Suzy would be interested in the detective stuff, and some of them featured drawings of space creatures that just looked too dumb. I finally settled on a copy of *True Confessions* and another one simply called *Secrets*. I realized that I was too embarrassed to actually take them up to the counter and buy them. The very front cover of one of them said in big orange letters "Who gave me VD?" What would the old men think of me? I carefully placed one on top of the other, so that the VD part wasn't showing. I fanned them so that the little boxes that said 35 cents were easy to see and bravely walked up to the counter.

"They're 35 cents each" I said, "I got two of em" I plopped two quarters and 2 dimes down on the counter.

"Found what you were looking for?" the man smiled at me and picked up the coins.

"Yes sir thanks." I quickly headed for the front door as the man walked around the counter and began to follow me. I could feel that he was walking right behind me. What did he want? Did he think I stole something? Was I in trouble for buying such weird magazines? I walked as quickly as I could, afraid that any second he would grab me by the back of the neck.

When I got to the door, he reached out his arm and pushed it open from behind me, "Goodnight young lady," he smiled and closed the door behind me. As I stepped outside and took a deep breath I heard the lock click behind me. What was I so afraid of? He was just walking me out so that he could close up. I rolled up the magazines and walked home.

After supper I called Suzy. "You wanna hear something really gross?" I whispered into the phone.

"What?"

"Meet me on my front porch and I'll tell you the story."

"Why don't you just tell me now?" Suzy asked

"Cause it's a long story and I don't want my Mom or Linda to hear."

I took the magazines and waited on the porch. The days were getting shorter and it was starting to get dark; I switched on the porch light so that we could see. Within a few minutes bugs were flying all around. I just managed to slap a mosquito before it bit my thigh when Suzy arrived.

"Check out this magazine, it has crazy stories about these girls who do all this weird sex stuff, and it's all true." I started to read her a story about the girl who was hitchhiking and got picked up by a guy who tied her up in the back seat of the car. She told him that she had to pee so he stopped at a gas station and let her use the bathroom. He threatened that he would kill her if she told anyone, so she didn't say anything. When she came out of the bathroom she complained real loud about how there was no toilet paper. When the gas station guy went in to replace the roll, he saw that she had used lipstick to write help and the license plate number on the mirror. He called the cops and they followed the car. Just as the guy was about to rip her clothes off, they rescued her.

"Cool, are all the stories like that?" Suzy asked as she waved a moth away from her face.

"Here, I got two, why don't you take this one." I handed her the *Secrets* magazine. "My Mother will kill me if she sees that VD story. Take it home and read it and you can tell me what it's about."

She flipped through the magazine, "Here's a good one: *I didn't want to die a virgin.* Wonder what that's all about."

I ran to the door and shut off the light. "Ugh, I can't stand it anymore. These bugs are driving me crazy. I'm going in. Here, take this one too." I handed her the other magazine.

"Cool, thanks. I'll bring em back tomorrow."

"No, that's okay; you can keep them. See you tomorrow." With that I went inside away from the bugs.

CHAPTER 19

"You got a birthday card," Linda said to me the next day as she brought the mail in. "Who's Trixie?"

"What? Let me see it," I said as I grabbed the small blue envelope from her hand. I stared at the envelope. It was addressed to Miss Margaret Ryan. My name and address were written with several different colors of markers. Hand drawn vines with little purple flowers bordered it. In the left hand corner was the return address, it wasn't from someone named Trixie, it read *T. Dixon.*

"It's from Trish. How does she know it's my birthday?" I thought back on our conversations, I never remembered discussing birthdays. Surely I would have remembered when hers was.

I carefully peeled open the flap, not wanting to destroy the artwork that scrolled around the entire envelope. I held it up to my face and sniffed. It smelled of the perfume that Trish had dabbed on my neck that day by the lake. Inside was not a birthday card, but a folded up piece of paper. The edge was rough, as if it had been torn out of a book. I recognized it as a page from Trish's journal.

I sat down on the front porch and unfolded it.

Dear Maggie,

You probably think I am a terrible friend, or maybe you don't think I am your friend at all. So let me start by saying I'M SORRY. I didn't mean to lie to you.

I made up the story about running away because I wanted us to have a special secret. I knew you were a real friend and would never tell anyone. You like mysteries and secrets, so I made up a story for you.

I guess you know that I live with my Grandma and Grandpa. My father died four years ago, that part was true. I really did live in Michigan for a while, that part is true too. I took the bus to your town each day because it was so nice there.

I hope you are not mad at me and will write back. You are my best friend and I had lots of fun with you in the summer. I hope you will forgive me and write me a letter. Maybe we can be pen pals. Maybe I can take the bus to visit again on a Saturday or maybe my Grandma can drive me. Please write back soon.

Love

xxxooo

Trish

P.S. Say hi to Suzy and Colleen.

I stared at the note, at Trish's neat

handwriting, the little flowers drawn in the margins, the x' and o's by the signature. She was sorry, that part was printed in big letters. She made up the story for me. She wanted us to have a special secret. She trusted me not to tell. How could I be mad at her? Suddenly I had a horrible thought. I wasn't worthy of her trust, I had given away her secret; I had told Carl and Mary Kay!

I tried to remember what had made me blab the secret. It just seemed like the thing to do at the time. Besides, I thought I would never see Trish again. I spent some time convincing myself that telling was the right thing to do. But there was still a little part of me that knew why I did it. I didn't want to admit it to myself, but I told Trish's secret so that I could feel closer to Carl.

The next day it really was my birthday. Suzy, Colleen and I went to the beach for what would be the last time that summer.

During our walk, Suzy started telling us a story, "So there's this kid who is so fat he can't get out of his room so his parents have him on a really strict diet. But the girl next door sneaks into his house every night and brings him all this food: potato chips and pizza and ice cream. They eat it all in his bed every night. His parents can't figure out why he is still so fat."

"Ugh, is this another one of your Uncle's stories?" Colleen asked.

"No, it's true. I read it in a magazine."

With that we all broke into song "You know I read it in a magazine." It was a line from the latest Elton John hit. We laughed and sang our way to the boardwalk.

Even though Suzy's story was gross, I was glad to hear it. I was sure it had come from one of the magazines I had given her. It meant she had actually read them!

We arrived at the badge checker and I stopped and stared at the quote.

The weak can never forgive; forgiveness is the attribute of the strong.

Mahatma Gandhi.

Water Temp 76: Hi Tide 3:10.

"This is a good one," I said, "and I've actually heard of the author." I thought about it for a minute. This might really mean something. Would I be strong and forgive Trish for lying to me? What about Suzy and her stealing? Most importantly I knew that Trish would forgive me for blabbing, because she was the strongest person I knew.

We spread out our towels and walked down to the water. Once we got out past the breakers, where the water was calm, I started to feel something strange on my skin. Something soft would occasionally brush against my legs.

Suzy raised up her hand and threw something at me. "Jellyfish!" she yelled just as the gelatinous blob went splat against my arm.

I peeled it off and threw it right back at her.

She ducked under the water and avoided being hit.

"Eww, I'm going in, I'm not getting stung," Colleen said as she headed toward shore.

"These are the clear ones, only the red ones sting," I told her.

"I don't care, they're gross and I'm getting out of here."

"C'mon Coll, this might be our last chance," I pleaded.

"Oh, let her go, Peggy, she's too mature for jellyfish fights." With that Suzy hurled a handful of goo right at my head. I dunked my head under to remove the slime from my hair and came up with two big handfuls of the slippery creatures. This time I caught Suzy off guard and landed a pile of jellies right on her chest.

"Nice throw!" Suzy laughed. "Watchin' all that baseball is finally paying off."

We played around in the water for a little longer, but each new wave seemed to bring in another crop of jellyfish. Eventually it was so thick with jellies that even Suzy was grossed out and we spent the rest of the day on the sand. At the end of our walk home I reminded my friends to come over after dinner for birthday cake.

That evening Colleen, Suzy, Cindy, Linda and I sat down in our dining room for cake and ice cream. My mother had made me a beautiful birthday cake. This year I had chosen a swan. It was covered with white coconut and decorated with bits of black licorice. It was both beautiful and delicious, well, except for the licorice parts. Luckily Linda loved licorice and was happy to eat the bits off of my slice.

My friends brought me gifts. I was nervous opening the little package from Suzy and Cindy. I did not want a gift they had stolen. They wouldn't really do that, would they? I was relieved to find several new tubes of seed beads. I knew they came from the tiny boutique in town where everything was behind a counter, they couldn't have stolen them. I now had every color of the rainbow; I right away planned to use them to make long necklaces like the ones Trish wore. Colleen gave me a little stained glass owl to hang in my bedroom window. I knew by the shape of my sister's gift that it was a book. But which book? I had long since returned Dinky Hocker to the library; did she buy me my own copy? I opened it and was delighted to see a leather-bound blank journal. It was the one we had seen at the stationers last month. It was perfect.

That night I sat on my bed with my new journal and some colored pencils. I knew exactly what I would do first. I started by drawing a beach scene along the bottom of the page, yellow sand and blue and green ocean waves. I drew a sun and some clouds and sea gulls near the top, but left plenty of room to write. I wanted the paper to be beautiful for my letter to Trish. I had forgiven her, and needed her to forgive me. I did my best to remember the wording of the quote on the blackboard. I wrote it in small letters near the bottom of the page, just inside the line of blue waves.

I composed my apology and invited her to visit soon. I told her that I wanted her to meet my new friends Mary Kay and Carl. I knew that when she met them, she would understand. I carefully tore out the page, put it in an envelope and put it out with the mail.

The next morning I had a plan. It did not include either Colleen or Suzy. First of all, Colleen wouldn't be caught dead at the Sheehan's bungalows, and Suzy, well; things didn't work out so great last time I took her there. I needed to talk to Carl and Mary Kay. I needed to explain that I should have never told them about Trish. I needed to know that they would keep our secret.

I put the cookie recipe in my back pocket, got on my bike and rode up to the bungalows. Things were very quiet. There was no music blaring from #602 and all of the other cabins looked deserted. When I turned my bike around the bend toward my friend's bungalow I saw Carl carrying a large cardboard box to the car.

He heard my bike tires on the gravel and looked up and smiled, "Hey Peggy, it's moving day! Did you come to help us?"

"You're moving out?"

"Yep, Labor Day is here and it's time to move back to the big house. I'm glad you found us before we left. C'mon."

I followed him into the house where Mary Kay was packing up the pots and pans from the kitchen. The little kitchen felt strangely empty. The big TV and the beautiful chair and tables were gone. The old couch sat by itself in the little living room. Without furniture, the place seemed to echo.

"Hi Peggy, do you want to help me pack up

the food?" She handed me a cardboard box and pointed toward the little cabinet. I carefully packed all the boxes of cereal and rice and other dry foods into the box. We finished packing up the kitchen and helped Carl load the boxes into the car until the trunk, the back seat and even the front seat were completely packed with their belongings.

"I guess I'm walking home darling," Carl said as he came back into the cabin after loading the very last box.

"Say goodbye to our summer home." He picked up Mary Kay and carried her down to the car.

I watched silently as he gave her a big kiss and she drove off down the gravel driveway.

"See you at home, Babe," she waved cheerily out from the car window.

I stood by the little front porch. I felt embarrassed that I was intruding on this tender moment between the two of them. I was also feeling something else, sort of sad and angry at the same time. I was jealous. Why couldn't it be me that Carl swept up in his arms?

As the car drove out of sight Carl turned to me. "So sweetheart, you gonna walk home with me?"

"I rode my bike." I nodded toward my bicycle which was leaning next to the bungalow.

"Well hop on!" Carl said as he grabbed the bike and held it for me by the handle bars.

I jumped on and he walked along side me, steering the bike with one arm. I put my feet on the pedals but I really wasn't pushing much. I let

Carl control our speed and direction as we traveled down the street. I thought that I should be nervous, but I wasn't; I felt completely safe and comfortable. I also felt completely happy. For that 15 minutes, Carl was all mine.

CHAPTER 20

"Carl," I said as we rolled along down Washington Avenue, "I turned 13 yesterday." It was almost a question.

"You had a birthday? Why didn't you say something? Well, Happy Birthday Peggy."

"Thanks." I blushed

"Did you have a party, a cake?"

I told him all about the swan cake and the gifts I had received. I described the blank book and told him about the letter I got from Trish.

"Well, I am so glad your friend Trish is OK. I got to admit, her story sounded a little fishy to me when you first told it. I guess Mary Kay was right. Some people just like to tell stories."

"Yeah, I'm kind of glad to know the truth now. I was worried about her. I just feel bad that I told you her secret. I promised not to tell. Do you think that makes me a bad friend?"

"Oh honey, no, you are definitely not a bad friend. Don't you remember how you went out in a storm to look for her? And look at how you took care of Suzy the other day. Oh, and let's not forget those cookies you brought us. Every time I see you, you are being a good friend to someone." He briefly let go of the handlebar and put his arm around my shoulder. He gave me a quick little hug and continued to push me down the block. We finished our journey in companionable silence.

"Here we are, home sweet home," Carl finally said as he pushed me up a white concrete driveway to a big yellow house just a block from the beach. Mary Kay's car was parked in the driveway in front of an oversized garage. The side door of the house was open.

Mary Kay came out and grabbed a box from the car.

"There you are," she smiled at us. "Just in time for me to take a break."

We unloaded the rest of the boxes and I helped Mary Kay put the food in the kitchen cabinets while Carl carried boxes upstairs. The house couldn't have been more different than the bungalow. It was big and bright with lots of large windows. It was an old house, but everything in it looked freshly painted and new. You could see the ocean from the screened-in front porch, and probably from the second floor rooms as well.

Carl finished moving things upstairs and came down, "It's got to be time for lunch. Aren't you two hungry?"

"I'll make some sandwiches," said Mary Kay, "You can show Peggy your workshop."

As soon as I walked into the workshop I recognized the scent, it was sweet with wood and saw dust. It was Carl; this is what he smelled like!

"I love the smell in here." I breathed in.

"Me too," Carl smiled, "Each wood had a different scent to it." He picked up a slab of wood from a table. "Smell this"

I sniffed the wood, "Mmm, Smells great."

"Red Oak." He handed me another piece, "Try this."

"Oh, that's kind of sharp or piney or something."

"Wow, you're good; it's pine"

"I never really thought about different kinds of woods before. What's this?" I picked up a small chunk of light colored wood. It had tiny spots in the grain. "It looks like it has a design in it."

"That's maple. They call it bird's eye because of the little burls in the grain. It grows that way. It's just a scrap left over from this chest." He pulled a cloth off of a table in the corner and revealed a large box. It was made with a darker wood with strips of the lighter maple set in. It was set on feet of spiraling squares. They were thicker, shorter versions of the wavy legs on the little table from the cabin.

"Wow! That is great. How did you get the legs to spiral like that?"

"Yeah, it's kind of tricky. I have to carve a lot of it by hand."

I walked around the big garage. There were several large machines with big sharp blades on them: electric saws and drills and stuff. There was also a workbench covered with hand tools. I looked up and saw a shelf covered with carved birds of all different shapes and sizes.

"Look at all the birds!" I exclaimed.

"Oh, those are just for fun, I whittle them from my scraps."

I realized that I was still holding the little chunk of maple, I opened my hand. "Like this?

You could turn this into a bird?"

"Sure, give me a couple of hours, and I'll make you something." He took the chunk from my palm.

"Oh, I didn't mean...I wasn't asking you to make me one!" I could feel my face turning red.

"Peggy, it's OK. I know you didn't ask. I am offering. I'll have it ready for you tomorrow."

With that we returned to the house and had lunch. I spent the afternoon helping to unpack their huge collection of records and put them in a specially designed cabinet in the living room.

As we said our goodbyes later that afternoon, Carl reminded me to stop by the next day.

I rode home feeling happier than I had in a long time. That evening I took off my shorts and found the folded up recipe card in my pocket. Once again I had forgotten to give it Carl. I looked at it. I would be embarrassed to give it to him now. It was all crinkled and worn from being near my butt all day. I went downstairs and found another index card. I very carefully rewrote it in my best printing.

As promised, I rode my bike to their house a the next day. The car wasn't in the driveway, so I almost rode right past without stopping. But then I noticed the side door to the workshop was open and there was music playing from inside. I stood in the doorway and watched as Carl cut a piece of wood on one of his big saws. He was wearing blue jeans and a tee shirt, his hair was pulled back in a pony tail. I had never seen him in his work clothes; I liked the way he looked. With his hair pulled back I could see the side of his face and his ear and his neck. I suddenly remembered the feeling I had when Trish rubbed the perfume on my neck. I reached my hand up and touched the soft skin of my own neck and earlobe.

The loud sound of the saw nearly drowned out the radio. I stared for a while as the man went about his work. I watched the muscles in his strong arms flexing as he picked up the planks of wood and cut them. He seemed totally focused on measuring and cutting, so much so that he didn't notice me standing there. After several minutes he stopped, looked up and smiled.

"Hi Carl, I didn't want to bother you. I brought you the cookie recipe."

"Hey Peggy. No bother, just starting a new project here. I guess I could use a little break."

I pulled the little recipe card out of my pocket and handed it to him.

"Cool, thanks! Mary Kay and I have to make a batch of these real soon."

We walked into the house and he poured two root beers. "Wait here just a sec," he said.

When he returned from the other room he was carrying a small package wrapped in blue tissue paper.

"Happy Birthday, a few days late." He handed me the gift.

I carefully unwrapped the paper to find a small wooden swan. It was made from the same speckled wood I had seen the day before. The wood was perfectly smooth and fit nicely into my hand. I turned it over in my palm and then held it to my nose to smell it.

"Does it smell OK?" Carl laughed.

"It's a swan. Did you really make this for me?"

"You told me about your swan cake, I thought you might like something that would last a little longer."

I felt a warm rush of feeling in my chest, for a second I thought I might cry. Then I did something without thinking. I reached out my arms and hugged him. He wrapped his arms around me for just a second. I breathed in the warm scent of cut wood and Carl. Then I remembered my manners

"Oh, thank you Carl, It's really cool. I love it"

He let me go. "You're welcome Peggy. I hope you enjoy it."

We finished our root beers and I left him to finish his work. I put the little swan in the front pocket of my jean shorts. I must have checked it a thousand times on the short ride home. Every time my right pedal came up, I put my hand on my right hip to make sure it was still there. I gave my new treasure a spot on my nightstand, right next to my bed.

The first day of school was upon us. Colleen and I walked to school together. We thought Suzy might walk with us, but we waited and she didn't come in time so we left without her.

"Late for school on the very first day. That's typical," said Colleen.

"Yep," I agreed, but wasn't so sure that Suzy was late. For all I knew, she might have gone in early. I didn't mention this, or the fact that Suzy would still be in the sixth grade; I wasn't sure if Colleen knew.

"Did you hear there's a new eighth grade teacher? Mrs. Fletcher left to have a baby."

"No, really? For my class or yours?" I asked. Colleen and I were never in the same class. They divided us into the A class and the B class. Colleen would be in 8B.

"You get the new one. Good luck."

I entered the classroom and looked around. I didn't have any close friends in the class, but there were a few girls that I would sometimes talk to. I sat near them in a seat by the windows. The new teacher was standing at the blackboard writing her name, Mrs. Ross. She was a thin woman with curly red hair; there was something familiar about her but I just couldn't place her. When she turned to the class and began to speak I pictured her, not in the flowered skirt and pink shell top that she was wearing, but in a striped track suit. I started giggling to myself. My new teacher was one of the Stripers! I had never seen her without her husband, or wearing anything but a jogging suit. "Wait 'till I tell Suzy" I thought.

Mrs. Ross introduced herself to the class and started taking attendance. The list of names was the same every year. I knew I would come right after Mark Rogers. She went through the list:

"Perry, Alice"

"Here"

"Rogers, Mark"

"Here"

"Ryan, Margaret"

I looked up and smiled, "Call me Maggie."

Quotations

Life shrinks or expands in proportion to one's courage. Nin, Anais: *The Diary of Anais Nin Volume 3,* 1939-1944

You can discover what your enemy fears most by observing the means he uses to frighten you. Hoffer, Eric: T*he Passionate State Of Mind, and Other Aphorisms* 1955

All things must change to something new, something strange. Longfellow, Henry Wadsworth: *Keramos and Other Poems* 1878

To the soul there is hardly anything more healing than friendship. Moore, Thomas

I've never known any trouble that an hour's reading did not assuage. De Secondat, Charles: *Mes Pensées (My Thoughts)* 1720–1755

There are some things you learn best in calm, and some in storm. Cather, Willa: *The Song of the Lark* 1915

All appears to change when we change. Amiel, Henri Frederic: *The Journal Intime* 1885

If you reveal your secrets to the wind, you should not blame the wind for revealing them to the trees. Gibran, Kahlil: *The Wanderer* 1932

The weak can never forgive. Forgiveness is the attribute of the strong.

Gandhi, Mohandes: *Young India* September 1924

Discussion Questions

1. Why does Peggy remain friends with Suzy and Colleen even when they are mean to her?

2. What should Peggy do when she discovers that Suzy has been shoplifting?

3. Trish has concocted an elaborate lie. Should Peggy continue to trust Trish when she finds out the truth?

4. This story was set in the 1970's. Could it take place in current times? What would be different today?

About the Author

Pat Heaney is an award-winning environmental educator who spends a great deal of her time outdoors with children. She grew up at the Jersey Shore and lives with her husband in New Jersey

Made in the USA
Charleston, SC
31 March 2014